Blur

(Night Roamers)

Book One

Kristen Middleton

Copyedited by:
Carolyn M. Pinard
www.thesupernaturalbookeditor.com

Cover Design – A collaboration by
Mae I Design and Emma Michaels
www.maeidesign.com
www.Emma Michaels.com

The characters and events portrayed in this book are fictitious. Any similarity to real persons, living or dead, is coincidental and not intended by the author.

To:

Dave, Cassie, and Allie

Your love inspires me…

Prologue

"Mom left the door unlocked," I hollered at my twin brother as he slammed the door to his '67 Mustang. It was the last day of eleventh grade, and we'd stopped off for burgers and malts at Grannie's Diner with some friends to celebrate after school. Nathan and I were officially seniors and neither of us could wipe the grins from our faces.

"That's weird," he said, brushing a hand through his sandy-brown hair. "You know how she's always nagging us about doing it."

I grinned and held the door open for him. "I'm certainly not going to let her live this one down."

Mom was married to a cop once, my father, and he'd drilled into her head how important it was to keep the doors locked, even when you're home.

Nathan followed me into the kitchen and opened the refrigerator.

"Oh, my God," I teased him. "How can you still be hungry after eating that monster burger and malt?"

He flexed a muscle. "I'm growing," he said. "Just 'cause you're a skinny little twerp doesn't mean everyone else has to eat like a bird."

I walked over and punched him in the arm. "Very funny."

He smiled and raised the milk carton to take a swig when we both heard it.

"What's that?" I whispered.

He slammed down the milk and rushed out of the kitchen.

"Nathan?" I yelled, chasing him upstairs. The sobs were coming from somewhere in the upper level of the house and my stomach twisted in horror.

Mom?

"Oh, my God," he choked, entering her dark bedroom. She was lying naked on the floor next to the bed, her face swollen and bleeding, her body badly bruised.

We rushed to her side and she cracked open one of her black eyes. "Call the police," she mumbled, barely coherent.

I started to cry as I grabbed the phone and dialed nine-one-one. I don't even remember talking to the person who'd answered. All I know is that I was blubbering and she was trying to console me with the fact that help was coming.

I hung up and stared at my broken mother in shock, feeling helpless and frightened. Thankfully, Nathan handled stress much better than I did.

He grabbed a comforter and covered her gently. "Mom, what happened?" he asked, pushing her dark bangs away from her eyes.

The shame on her face was heart-wrenching and I pretty much knew by her appearance what had happened. She'd obviously been beaten and raped.

I brushed the tears from my face, kneeled down next to her, and lightly touched her hand. "The police and ambulance are on their way."

She nodded and closed her eyes.

"Mom?" prodded Nathan. "What happened?"

"Nathan, think about it," I whispered. "She's been raped."

His lips trembled as he searched her face. "Mom, some stranger broke in here and... did this?"

She opened her eyes and stared at both of us for a few seconds. "No... no stranger," she whispered hoarsely. "It was your father."

Chapter One

"Are we almost there?" I asked, staring through my sunglasses at the endless rows of cornfields. We'd been driving for hours through the countryside and I could no longer tell the difference from one town to the next. More than anything, I just wanted to get out of the car and stretch my legs, which were starting to tingle in an uncomfortable way.

Mom cleared her throat. "Pretty soon."

Nathan was following us in his Mustang and I glanced back to see him talking on his cell phone once again.

"Oh, Lord," I said, leaning my head back against the headrest. "He must be talking to Deanna for the tenth time. She just won't get over the fact that we're really moving."

Mom tightened her hands on the steering wheel and glanced at me. "I'm sorry about this. I'm just so sorry… about everything."

I groaned. "Mom, for crying out loud, it's not your fault. I can't even believe you're feeling guilty about it. I mean, nobody had any idea that he could be so violent."

It had been less than three months since my father had brutally attacked my mother. They'd been separated for the last couple of years because of his sporadic temper tantrums, along with his inability to stop screwing other women. When my mother had finally gotten up the nerve to leave him, surprisingly, he'd actually been pretty civil about it. Then, when he'd found out she'd moved on emotionally and started dating again, he'd went off in a jealous rage, striking back at her viciously. We were all still stunned about the horrifying ordeal.

"I just wish they could locate him," she said, staring straight ahead. "He's... crazy."

I nodded. I was so ashamed, that any thoughts of him made me physically ill. It was still really hard to believe that my own father was capable of being so violent, especially since he'd been a cop and responsible for keeping people safe. After the attack, he'd disappeared, and my poor mother had spent several nights in the hospital recovering. When she finally came home, she wasn't able to sleep at night without drugs, terrified that he'd show up and beat her again. Then, just recently, she'd been given a gift; a way out. Her employer offered her an accounting job in Montana and that's where all three of us were now headed; to start a new life.

"I think it's good that Nathan's getting away from Deanna anyway," I said, staring in dismay at my short, stubbly nails. Not that they'd been perfect before, but all of the packing and cleaning had taken its toll. "She's so whiny and annoying."

Mom smiled wryly. "Now, Nikki, you haven't liked any of Nathan's girlfriends."

"It's not my fault he attracts the psycho ones."

She burst out laughing and I smiled, enjoying a sound that was finally finding its way back into our lives again.

"God, you're awful," she said, shaking her head in amusement.

I snorted. "Oh, come on. You know I'm right."

She grabbed her Ray-Bans from the center column and plopped them onto her nose. "Yeah, he's a little too young to be tied down to just one girl. So if you ask me, this move will be healthy for the both of them."

"Oh, I'm sure Deanna will find someone else by next week anyway." I made a face. "She's so freaken needy."

"You really don't like her, do you?"

I shrugged.

Deep down, I knew I wasn't being totally fair, because the truth was, I was a little jealous. My brother and I had always been very close, especially living in such a dysfunctional family environment. My earliest memories were of my parents screaming and fighting, especially during the holidays. So, we'd weathered the storms together. In fact, for all of our lives, we'd been best friends; sharing and doing everything together. That is, until the tenth grade, when he'd discovered boobs, I mean girls. Of course I'd discovered boys as well; I'd discovered that most of them in my school were crude, boring, or just plain boobs.

"So, mom," I said, changing a subject in which, I had to admit, left me feeling a little guilty. "What were you saying about this place we're renting?"

She grinned. "I guess it's just beautiful. It's a cabin on Shore Lake that's been on the market for some time. The owners are related to Ernie, and because of our circumstances; they're letting us stay there relatively cheap."

Ernie was my mom's boss; a really nice old man who's been very supportive. He's been like a father-figure to her, which is good because both of her parents passed away several years ago, and aside from us, she doesn't have anyone else.

"A cabin sounds really cool. Do they happen to have a boat?"

"Yes, actually, and Ernie says he's caught *hundreds* of fish on the lake, so we've got to check it out. I'm really excited about staying there. Honey, are you okay?"

"Something in my eye," I muttered as I pulled down the visor. I blinked until I finally got the eyelash out.

I touched my long, unruly hair and frowned. It had been almost six months since I'd last had it cut; now it was down to my lower back and I was constantly fighting snarls. "Jeez, I could really use a haircut."

She put a hand on my shoulder and squeezed. "Don't worry, honey. We'll get you one before school starts. Once I get some extra money, you know?"

"Sure."

I bit my lower lip and examined my reflection. Sandy brown hair, light blue eyes, and a pug nose. I'd always considered myself average looking, even though my mom said I looked exactly like her when she was growing up, and she turned out to be attractive. In fact, most of Nathan's friends said she was a hot MILF, which *was* pretty gross, but I guess that meant there was still hope for me.

I closed the visor and leaned my head back against the seat. "I wonder what the school is like."

I was definitely a little nervous about going to a new school, although, truthfully, I knew I wouldn't particularly miss the old one much. In fact, you could say I was sort of a loner. Sure, there were a couple of girls I'd hung out with back home occasionally, but I preferred to be alone most of the time, or hanging out with Nathan.

"Ernie didn't say much, but honestly, I don't expect him to know. He's in his seventies and never had children."

"I'm sure it will be fine."

I really didn't want my mom to worry about me. She was the one who needed the extra support from us and I wasn't about to make her feel any more guilty about moving than she already did.

She slapped her fingers on the steering wheel. "Oh, I forgot to tell you, they have a computer, so you can surf the Internet."

"Really? That's cool," I smiled. Although we used computers at school and my mom had her own laptop, I'd been nagging her forever about getting me one of my own.

"Yes, but you'll have to share it with your brother. I'd let you guys use mine, but…"

I smirked. "I know, you have too many important files and you don't want anything happening to your computer."

"Now *you* have one to use," she answered. "And I won't have to listen to you two badger me about it, anymore."

"At least I can download books from the library," I replied. "We'll be in the middle of nowhere out here and I'll need something to do."

"Oh, I'm sure you'll find plenty of things to do. Wait until you start school and meet some new friends. Or," her face lit up, "maybe even some cute boys."

I rolled my eyes. "Right. I doubt very much that's going to happen."

"Why in Heaven's name would you say that? You're a very pretty girl, Nikki. Don't sell yourself short."

The truth was, I couldn't care less about meeting anyone at the moment. Most of the girls at my old school had been constantly stressed out because of their immature boyfriends and I wasn't about to go down that road, especially in my last year of high school. "It doesn't matter."

She frowned. "Sure it does. You'll want to go to all the dances, and then there's the prom. You don't want to miss out on all the fun. You'll regret it later."

"Didn't you go with dad to the prom?" I asked, then immediately felt rotten when I saw the bitterness reflected in her eyes.

"I did," she said slowly. "But, he wasn't always so… volatile. And, really, he's among the very few out there like that. You know, Nikki, you can't be afraid of the world because your dad has some issues."

13

Yeah, but weren't we running because she was still very much afraid?

Of course, I didn't dare mention that. Instead, I just changed the subject.

"So, how much farther of a drive do we have, mom?" I asked, noticing the mountains coming up in the distance.

"Oh, just a couple more hours," she replied, plugging in her iPod. Seconds later, Adele, began to sing about *Rumors*.

I stretched my arms and yawned.

"Honey," she said, lowering her sunglasses, "you look beat; why don't you try and get some rest? I'll wake you when we get there."

"Okay," I said, closing my eyes. "Maybe I'll just take a little nap."

~~~

"Why not, mom? I just don't understand," protested Nathan.

She sighed. "Can we *please* talk about Deanna later?"

I woke up to the sound of mom and Nathan arguing. We were parked by a small grocery store and he was standing outside of her window, pouting.

"Oh God, not now," I mumbled. It was getting dark and we'd missed dinner and my stomach was protesting. I was cranky, and the last thing I needed was to hear any more drama about Deanna.

"Can't she just come for a week before school starts?" said Nathan. "She's having a rough time with her parents, and now that I'm gone, things have gotten even worse. It's not fair for her."

She shook her head. "No, we have too much to do with unpacking and getting ready for school. Maybe she can come and visit sometime after it starts for a weekend."

14

"This is all bullshit," he snapped, backing up from the window. He raised his hands in exasperation. "We could have stayed home. I would've protected you. Now we're forced to move, and you didn't even give me a chance."

"Nathan!" I gasped. "You are the one not being fair. Mom's been through so much and you're just mad because you can't see Deanna whenever you want. God, you're being an asshole."

His face turned red and he opened up his mouth to retaliate when mom quickly interrupted.

"Okay, let's all settle down. Quit pointing fingers at each other, and Nikki, watch your mouth."

"Sorry," I mumbled.

"Listen, it isn't either of your faults, okay? And, Nathan," she said, smiling sadly, "I'm grateful that you want to protect me, but you can't possibly follow me around twenty-four hours a day, nor do I expect you to be my personal bodyguard. Now, as far as Deanna goes, we'll talk about it later. Comprende?"

He nodded but was still sulking and I could tell that this conversation was far from over.

She noticed it as well and rubbed her forehead in frustration. "Okay, let's get the things we need in the grocery store before it gets dark. I don't want to get lost while searching for this cabin."

"Let's go," I said, opening my door.

Nathan followed us into the store, still moping.

"Nathan, would you please cheer up?" she pleaded when we were in the frozen pizza section and he refused to pick out food.

"Yeah," I said. "Don't ruin our first night here because of a girl who's probably lining up her next soul-mate as we speak."

"Would you just *shut-up*?" he snapped. "You're just jealous because you didn't leave anyone behind that mattered."

I took a step towards him. "Excuse me? Jealous!?"

"Stop it!" hissed mom, getting into both of our faces. "We're in public and you're both acting... ridiculous. Now, I'm sorry that we had to move, I really am. But we're here now and there's no turning back. So get it together, or I swear to God, I won't buy any ice cream."

Nathan raised his hands in the air. "Okay, mom, just settle down. We can talk about this, no need to bring ice cream into the equation. That's cruel."

She smirked. "That's what I thought." She then turned to me. "What about you? Are you going to lay off Deanna, who isn't even here to defend herself?"

"Fine," I replied tightly. "As long as he stops talking about her every five minutes."

"Whatever," he replied, shaking his head.

She closed her eyes and rubbed the bridge of her nose. "You know, maybe this was a mistake, I don't know." She opened her eyes. "But, what's done is done, *and* we have to make the best of it. So, please, quit arguing and let's try to make the best of this. Okay?"

We both agreed, but avoided eye contact.

"Okay," she said, smiling again. "Now, let's finish this up and find the cabin. I think you're going to really like living out here if you just give it a chance. I mean, come on, you have to admit – the scenery is beautiful."

"California was beautiful too," replied Nathan, grabbing a stack of pizzas from the freezer. "I'm just saying..."

She rolled her eyes. "Seriously?"

He put the pizzas in the cart. "Okay, fine, I'll admit that it's different here – the fresh air, the mountains, all of the greenness. I guess it's cool."

"Thank you. Now, let's grab some Hot Pockets and Pizza Rolls," she said, staring at the case.

I grimaced. "Hot Pockets?"

She motioned her thumb at Nathan. "We need to keep him fed. Those are quick and easy."

It was true, he was always hungry, and once his blood sugar began to drop, grumpier than all hell. Our dad's family was prone to Diabetes and mom predicted we'd both end up getting it someday.

I opened the glass door and began sorting through the Hot Pockets with Nathan directing. Forty-five minutes later, the entire cart was full and Deanna was temporarily forgotten.

"That will be two-hundred-and-forty dollars," said the cashier, snapping her gum.

Mom handed the young woman her credit card while the cashier appraised Nathan as he bagged the groceries. When he finished, she smiled. "Thanks. You didn't have to do that, you know. It's my job."

"That's okay. I don't mind."

"You guys just move here?" she asked, twirling a piece of her blonde hair around her index finger.

I refrained from rolling my eyes.

"We did," smiled my mother. "Just today, in fact."

"Cool," replied the girl, still staring at him like he was a pair of designer jeans that she couldn't possibly live without. "See you around."

"Yeah," replied Nathan as he began to push the grocery cart outside without a backwards glance.

Mom and I looked at each other in amusement. Sometimes men were so clueless.

"Let's put the groceries in *your* car, Nathan," said mom as we stepped back outside. "Mine is too full already."

"Okay," he replied, veering towards his vehicle.

As we were trying to stuff the food into the back of Nathan's Mustang, a soft voice greeted us. "Hi. You must be new in town?"

We all turned around to see a striking redhead getting out of a tall Chevy pickup. She wore a miniscule white sundress, which showed off her toned legs, and dark sunglasses, which I thought was a little odd, considering it was dusk.

Nathan's blue eyes lit up and he grinned. "Yeah, we just pulled into town."

She removed her sunglasses and smiled back. "I hope you enjoy it here. It's quaint, but there are lots of things to do, especially after dark."

Her teeth were pearly white and her hair was a mass of shiny curls. She dropped her keys, and after she bent to retrieve them, tossed her hair back over her shoulder. It was a simple thing, but it had an immediate effect on Nathan. Truthfully, I didn't think anybody should be that gorgeous.

Before my mother or I could get in a word, Nathan spoke up in a surprisingly deeper voice. "Thanks for the info. Maybe we'll run into each other sometime."

"Maybe. It was really nice meeting you," she replied, clearly directing it towards Nathan, who looked like he'd all but forgotten about Deanna. Then she sashayed into the store like a runway model while we all stared.

"Wow," I smirked, turning towards my brother. "You can reel your tongue back in now."

"What do you mean?"

I snorted. "Oh, come on, Nathan."

He smiled innocently. "There's nothing wrong with being friendly to strangers, especially when they look like that."

"I think the feeling was mutual," replied mom, looking at me. "That smile she gave him was enough to light up the entire town."

"How can she resist?" he said cockily. "Heck, I'll bet that I'm the best thing that's ever walked into this town."

I rolled my eyes. "Oh, Lord. Here we go."

He flexed left arm muscle. "Oh, come on, you know I'm right."

"I certainly do," said mom, leaning over to kiss his cheek.

"Yeah, and mom's biased," I replied. "Don't let it go to your head."

He ignored me and started packing more groceries into the back of his trunk. "Let's get the rest of this stuff loaded quickly," he said, glancing up towards the sky, which was growing darker. "I'm starving and it's getting late."

"Me too," I replied, handing him another bag of groceries.

When we had everything in the trunk, Mom gave Nathan the directions to the cabin, which was a few miles past town, and this time, he led the way.

"Finally," I said, putting on my seatbelt as she pulled out of the parking lot. "I just want to get there already."

"Won't be long now."

Darkness came very quickly, and in a small town without many lights along the roads, it was a little creepy.

"It's a bitch driving when you don't know exactly where you're going in the dark," said mom, frowning. "I think the turnoff is coming up in another few miles or so. I hope Nathan catches it in time and doesn't overshoot it."

"Knowing him, he probably will," I answered with a smirk, "especially, if he's on the phone with Deanna again."

"He seemed to forget about her when that redhead made an appearance."

"Thank God, although, she's probably worse than Deanna."

"Let's hope not."

I stared at her in shock. "See, you weren't crazy about her either!"

She turned down the radio. "Are you kidding me?" she groaned, scowling into the rearview mirror.

I turned to see the flashing lights from a police car. "What, were you speeding or something?"

She pulled over to the side of the road. "No, you know me, I never speed."

It was true, my mother was an annoyingly slow driver and Nathan was always giving her crap about it. Even grandmothers passed *her* on the roadway.

Mom rolled down the window as the police officer approached her. She immediately handed him her driver's license and insurance information. "I'm sorry, officer... was I speeding?"

My brother had noticed the cop, too, and pulled over ahead of us, waiting. He'd sent me a text message, wondering what was happening. I'd sent him one back, explaining that I wasn't really sure, yet.

"No, but you do have a taillight out," he replied with an easy smile.

My eyes widened as I stared at his mouth. *What's with this town and their unnaturally white teeth?*

"Oh, no, really?" she answered, biting her lower lip. "Oh, man, I'm sorry. It must have just went out."

"Yes. Anne Gerard... you must be new in town?" he asked, studying her license.

She smiled. "We are, in fact," she pointed towards me, "this is my daughter, Nikki, and that's my son, Nathan, ahead of us in the Mustang."

He glanced down at her left hand, which no longer had a wedding ring, and his smile broadened.

"Ladies, I'm Sherriff Caleb Smith. Welcome to Shore Lake," he answered, giving her back her license.

Was it me or did he actually puff out his chest a little before he leaned back down and handed it back?

"Thank you," answered my mom with a silly grin on her face. She definitely noticed the puff.

"Since you have such a lovely smile and you're new in town, I'm just going to give you a warning. Make sure that you take care of it as soon as you can, though. Next time I might not be so easy on you."

Mom smiled wider than ever. "I will, thank you, officer."

He tipped his hat. "My friends call me Caleb. Drive safely now."

"Wow," said mom after she'd rolled up her window. "Did you see that man's eyes? They were an amazing shade of violet. I don't think I've ever seen anyone with that color of eyes. No wedding ring, either."

I stared at her in disbelief. "Oh, my God mom, we *just* got into town!"

"Yeah, but I agree with Nathan that there's nothing wrong with making new friends; especially friends who are in law enforcement," she replied with a straight face.

"Well, I guess," I answered, staring into the darkness. Obviously, she was beginning to get a handle on her fears and I should have been relieved, but instead, it only made me… uneasy.

Chapter Two

When we finally made it to the cabin, my jaw literally dropped.

"What do you think?" asked mom as she parked the car next to Nathan's.

"Wow. It's amazing," I replied, opening the car door. "Are you sure this is the right place?"

"It is. I saw pictures but wanted to surprise you," she said, getting out of the car.

This was no average lakeside cabin; it looked like something you'd see on a "Top Ten List" of some luxurious getaways.

"This must be worth millions. I can't believe we're staying here," I said, unable to wipe the grin from my face. I felt like someone had just shouted "Move that bus!" and we were looking at our new dream home.

"Yes, it's quite extraordinary," she said, staring up at the cabin. "I'm still in shock that we get to stay here, too. Ernie is a lifesaver."

"He's more like Santa Claus," I replied, feeling giddy. I couldn't wait to check out the inside. It was possible that Shore Lake wasn't going to suck quite as much as I thought.

She reached back into the car and pulled out her cell phone. "I'd better call him once we've unpacked the groceries. Let him know we've made it and how thrilled we are." Her eyes became misty. "You know, I just can't thank him enough for everything he's done."

I agreed with her there. This place was beyond words. Heck, everything about it screamed money, too, from the expensive cedar wood frame to the thick-plated enormous glass windows; it reminded me of a mountainside chateau in Europe.

"Impressive, huh?" she said.

"Yeah."

Especially with its two-tiered deck that someone had built on north side of the cabin, and a massive porch that wrapped around the entire main floor. There was even a gazebo with a hot tub next to a courtyard which contained a large grill and several pieces of outdoor furniture for entertaining. Unfortunately, we had nobody to entertain.

"Wow," said Nathan as he got out of the car and walked over to us. He was also staring in amazement at the cabin. "How in the world did you score such an awesome place?"

Mom smiled. "Ernie."

"Look, there's the boathouse." I pointed down towards the lake. Even that place looked like it was larger than some of the homes in our old neighborhood.

"Cool," said Nathan, nodding in approval. "I hope the weather is nice tomorrow, so that we can take the boat out," he started walking towards the dock. "I wonder what kind of boat they have?"

"Check later," said mom, grabbing her purse. "We need to get this stuff inside."

He sighed and turned around. "Okay. It's probably too dark to see anything now anyway."

She took the keys out of her purse and began walking towards the cabin. "You know, I'm really surprised that there isn't some kind of alarm on the cabin. I mean, this place is vacant most of the time." She sighed. "I hope when we get inside, nothing is missing."

"Everyone must trust each other in these parts," I said, following her up the steps to the front door.

"Apparently," she answered, putting the key into the lock. When we stepped inside, she flipped on the lights and my breath caught in my throat.

"Wow..." said Nathan. "This place is... tight."

"It's amazing," she said, taking a step back. "I'm just, speechless."

"Can we step inside of the doorway, people?" I said, swatting at a mosquito. "Before the bugs enter before we do?"

"Oh, sorry," she chuckled.

We entered what had to be called the "great room." It was enormous and had a large soapstone fireplace with a bearskin rug lying near it, which was kind of hokey to me but it certainly added to the affect. Plush burgundy colored leather furniture with hand-carved wooden end tables sat across from the fireplace, and I imagined myself in the chair-and-a-half, reading a book next to a crackling fire.

"Wow, I just love those light fixtures," gushed mom, staring at the dozens of rustic chandeliers that made the place glow with warmth. She walked over to a row of intricately carved shelves and touched the amber colored wood. "And all of this lovely hand-carved woodwork, the leather furniture, and... oh God, what isn't there to love about this place? Next time I see Ernie, I'm going to plant a huge kiss on his little bald head."

"You should," said Nathan. He raised his voice a few octaves and put a hand on his hip. "And give him a big sloppy one from me, too."

"Oh, so you're finally warming up to us being here?" she asked.

He grinned. "Mom, seriously, if you're happy, then I'm happy."

She walked over to Nathan and threw her arms around him. "I swear, I have the two best kids in the world."

"Love you, too, mom," he answered, patting her gently on the back. "And don't worry, everything will work out. Even… even with Deanna. Seriously."

"Good, I'm glad you feel that way," she replied, releasing him. "I just want everything to work out for you and your sister."

"Don't worry. I'm sure it will," he replied.

"Guys, I'm going to check out the upstairs," I said, climbing the staircase, two steps at a time. I could barely contain my excitement now that I knew we were actually staying at such a glamorous place.

"Pick out a bedroom!" she called as I made it to the top of the stairs. "I don't care which; I hear they're all pretty nice."

"Will do!" I hollered back.

There were several bedrooms on the upper level, all spacious and each having their own bathroom. I chose one with a queen-sized pillow-top bed and a small balcony with an awesome view of the lake.

"So, what do you think?" asked my mom from the doorway, a few minutes later.

"Oh, my God, I love it!" I squealed. "I feel like we're on vacation somewhere. I wish we could stay here forever."

"I know, it's pretty breathtaking. I don't know about this one, but my bedroom has its own Jacuzzi and a closet so big, I could park the car in it. I'm going to check out yours."

While she did that, I walked over to the balcony door and opened it, enjoying the cool air on my cheek. It was dark outside, but the reflection of the moon on the water made the lake seem so peaceful. I imagined myself lying on some kind of canoe or boat, staring up at the moon with the waves rocking me to sleep. "I just can't believe this place. If we're dreaming, I never want to wake up."

She stepped next to me and linked her arm through mine. "Don't worry, it's real."

My stomach began to growl and I patted it. "I don't know about you, but I'm starving."

"Yeah, I'm getting there myself. Let's go see if Nathan did what I asked and brought the groceries inside. I'll make us something to eat."

"Okay."

We went back downstairs and I helped mom put the rest of the groceries away in the fridge, which actually looked like the wooden cupboards surrounding it.

She took out a frying pan from one of the boxes in the kitchen and smiled. "Who wants homemade sliders? It might be ghetto here, but I'm not about to give those up."

"Yeah, I'll take as many as you can make," replied Nathan as he entered the kitchen. "I'm going to pass out if I don't get something to eat soon."

"I'm surprised you're still walking," I said.

"Me too," he said, opening up the refrigerator. He grabbed a jar of pickles and untwisted the cap. Before he could get his fingers inside of the jar, mom stopped him.

"Here," she said, handing him a fork. "Don't use your fingers."

He grinned sheepishly. "Oh, thanks."

"So," she said as she began preparing dinner, "is this place incredible or what?"

"Not too shabby," said Nathan between bites of his pickle. "And it's so quiet, I feel like we're in the middle of nowhere."

Mom nodded. "The next cabin is just a hop, skip, and a jump from here, but you'd never know it's so peaceful."

"Yeah, you did good, mom," I said, cutting the onions for our burgers. "I just can't wait until tomorrow when we get to see it all in the daylight."

Nathan nodded. "Yeah, I'd really like to take the boat out on the lake tomorrow, if that's okay?"

"Sure," she answered

He wiped his hands on his jeans. "Sweet."

She opened the fridge and grabbed the cheese. "I think that would be good for all of us to get out on that lake. I haven't been able to work on my tan all summer."

I snorted; my mom was as white as a ghost and typically burned and peeled, but never really tanned. My brother and I were the opposite, fortunately, even though you'd never know it this year. I just hadn't had the time to get any sun, especially after the "incident."

After dinner, I helped her with the dishes and then decided to check out the whirlpool tub in my bathroom.

"I'm taking a long, relaxing bath and then going to bed," I said as we neared the staircase. It had been a long drive and I was so exhausted, I didn't even feel like unpacking anything just yet.

"Okay," she replied, kissing the top of my head. "I'll see you in the morning."

A moving company had dropped off our belongings earlier in the day and I found some of my own boxes very quickly. After carrying them to my room, I grabbed a towel and the fluffy white robe my mom had given me for Christmas last year. As I was about to walk into my bathroom to start the tub, there was a soft knock.

"Yeah?"

My brother opened the door. "Hey, I'm sorry about snapping at you earlier. You were right," he said with a sheepish grin. "I was being a little bit of an asshole."

"Don't worry, I'm used to it."

He folded his arms across his chest. "You were kind of a bitch too, you know."

I gasped. "I'll show you bitch," I replied, throwing my hairbrush at him. It missed and hit the wall next to the door.

"Better work on your aim," he replied with a smirk.

I picked up my curling iron and raised it in the air. "Leave before I give you ringlets! I swear to God, I'll make you pretty!"

He brushed his bangs away from his eyes. "Can you include a bow? I'd look even prettier with a bow."

I broke down and started laughing. "You are such a freak."

"No need to be jealous. You're my twin and kind of a freak, too."

"Lucky me."

He smiled. "Night, Nik. I'll see you in the morning."

"Okay, goodnight."

After he left, I grabbed my things and stepped into the black and white marbled bathroom, locking the door behind me. When I turned back around, I smiled.

Amazing.

There was even a large panoramic window surrounding the Jacuzzi with a view of the lake. Although it was dark and I couldn't see much of anything outside, I imagined during the day, it was incredible.

I walked over to the large square tub and turned on the water. I sat on the edge and watched it rise slowly, wondering how many gallons I'd be using before it covered the jets entirely. It was enormous, even larger than the pool we'd had as kids. Hell, the entire bathroom was fit for a celebrity and I was going to use it for the next year or two? I decided to kiss Ernie myself the next time I saw him.

I stood back up and opened the new vanilla-scented spa bath gift set my mom had given me. I then lit the candle that came with it and placed it near the tub. When the water was high enough, I pulled my hair back into a ponytail, turned off the lights, and removed my shirt and jeans.

"Oh, yeah, now that's what I'm talking about," I whispered, groaning in pleasure as I sunk into the warm bath. I laid my head against the bath pillow and closed my eyes. I imagined it couldn't possibly get any better, but then remembered I'd forgotten my iPod. If this was Heaven, then listening to the music could only take me to another level of bliss.

As I stood up to grab a towel, my eyes were drawn towards a movement near the right side of the window that I was now facing. My heart stopped as a set of fiery-red eyes stared back at me. When I finally found my voice, I screamed in horror, and whatever it was, quickly shot away.

"Mom!" I shrieked, trying not to slip on the wet floor. I grabbed my robe and skidded out of the bathroom as quickly as possible.

"What is it?" she cried, bursting through the door, also wearing her yellow terrycloth robe.

Trembling, I pointed towards the bathroom. "Mom," I choked, "someone was watching me in the window! They saw me naked!"

Her eyes widened and she reached for the softball bat sticking out of one of my boxes. With my heart pounding in my chest, I followed her into the bathroom, half expecting someone to jump out of the shadows. She kept the light switch off and moved towards the window.

"Do you see anything?" I whispered over her shoulder.

Sighing, she turned to me and lowered the bat. "No."

I looked back towards the darkness, and a shiver ran down my spine. I turned back to her. "Are you sure?"

Her forehead wrinkled. "Yes, I'm sure. I also don't see how anyone could be watching you from this height, Nikki."

"Mom, something was watching me. I'm not lying."

She touched my cheek. "Baby, it's been a long day and we're in the middle of the woods. You probably saw a bird flying by – or maybe even a bat. Don't be frightened."

My bedroom *was* several feet from the ground, and truthfully, I really wasn't sure what I'd seen. Obviously, it had to be some kind of animal. "I guess that's possible."

She held out a hand to me. "Come here and see for yourself. Look how far up we really are."

Of course, when I looked back outside, common sense told me that we were too high for any person to be looking in.

I closed my eyes. "Yeah, okay, maybe it was just a stupid bat or something."

"Honey, you're obviously very tired. Why don't you go to bed and get a good night's sleep? I'll bet that tomorrow, you'll be laughing about this."

"Is everything okay in here?" asked Nathan, standing in the doorway in his blue flannel pajama pants.

"Everything's fine," she answered with another reassuring smile. "Nikki just saw a bird or something outside and it scared the hell out of her."

Nathan's eyebrows shot up. "Seriously? You know, I thought I saw something out there, too, when I was in my room watching TV. It freaked the shit out of me."

I turned to see her reaction.

"What?" she asked, staring at both of us, amused. "Come on… it's some kind of bird. You know, there's no possible way a living person could stand outside of your bedroom windows and look in. Unless Spider-man is vacationing in Montana and has decided to scale this particular cabin to check us out. You two are wigging out over nothing."

"Still, I think we should take a look outside," said Nathan as he turned and walked away.

"Wait!" my mom hollered. She picked up the bat and charged after him. "Don't go out there without this!"

And she thought I was being paranoid?

I followed them both downstairs and watched as he switched on the outdoor lights and threw open the front door.

"Be careful!" I hollered, staying back. There was no way I was going out into that unknown darkness, harmless bird or not.

My mom hesitantly followed Nathan outside while I wrapped my arms around myself, trying to remain calm under the circumstances.

This is crazy, I thought, when they closed the door behind them. I wondered if it really was some kind of large bird checking both of us out. Maybe an owl or eagle?

But with red eyes?

Owls were nocturnal so I imagined it was possible, although, I was a city girl and didn't know the first thing about birds, other than they pooped, *a lot*, whenever they felt like it.

I chewed on my lower lip and stared towards the dark windows, suddenly wondering if someone or something was watching me from the other side.

Oh, my God… close the blinds, idiot!

I leaped towards the windows, moving the wooden blinds over the four large plated windows as quickly as possible. Once they were all covered, I took a step back and began breathing again.

While I waited for my mom and brother to return, I couldn't help it, I began to pace as the anxiety quickly built up again. I was definitely wigging out just like she'd said. I started imaging things like Sasquatches and aliens, freaking myself out until I felt like I was almost to the point of hyperventilating.

31

Jesus, Nikki, chill the hell out.

Frustrated, I went back over to the sofa and sat down, tapping my foot nervously. Seconds later, my brother stormed through the front door, followed by my mom, whose face was as pale as the moon. He picked up the phone and started dialing.

My stomach tightened when I noticed the strange look on Nathan's face. "Okay, what's going on?"

Nathan raised his hand to silence me and then began speaking, his voice strangled. "Hello? Yes, I'd like to report a dead body."

Chapter Three

Three hours later, the dead body, which they'd found near the dock, was examined, bagged, and finally taken away.

"Well," said Sheriff Caleb Smith, who was standing on the porch. "It looks like it's the teenage girl who's been missing for a few weeks, Tina Johnson."

"What happened to her?" I asked, staring at him. He was taller than I'd thought, standing well over six-foot, had dark hair that hung just below his collar, and an almost perfectly chiseled face, except for his nose, which was a little large. I had to admit, though, for a guy in his thirties, he was handsome.

My mother, who was staring up at him as if he was Superman, cleared her throat. "Before you answer that, would you like to come in and have a cup of coffee, Sheriff?"

He grinned widely and stepped inside. "Thanks; don't worry about the coffee, though. I really need to be leaving soon."

"So, was she murdered?" asked Nathan, still freaked out about finding her bloated body sticking out of the water. He'd described it so many times to me that I could see the image in my head, as if I'd actually been there.

The sheriff shook his head. "I don't think so. She had a history of drinking and left a party pretty intoxicated at the time she went missing. She may have simply fallen into the water and drowned. There will be an autopsy, however, so we'll know more later."

Nathan, who watched a lot of C.S.I. shows on television, crossed his arms over his chest. "So, there were no witnesses? Nobody at the party actually saw her leave?"

The sheriff put his hand on the wall and leaned against it. "No. That particular party got a little out of hand and we ended up arresting a few minors for intoxication that night. It was an ugly mess."

"Goodness," said mom. "What a horrible thing for her parents. I can't imagine what it's been like for them."

He nodded, looking very somber. "Just like us, they've been frantically searching for her all over this town and the next ones over. Well," he sighed, "at least they have some closure now."

"How tragic; I can't possibly imagine how I'd cope in their situation," she said.

He nodded. "I agree."

"Sherriff, are you sure you wouldn't like a cup of coffee? It'll just take a minute to brew."

"No, Anne, but thanks again for the offer." He straightened up and patted his pockets, as if searching for his keys. "I'd better get going; my daughter's expecting me home soon."

"You have children?" she asked.

He smiled proudly. "A daughter, Celeste. She just graduated."

"Oh, you're a single parent?" she asked, smiling as if she'd just won big on a lottery scratch-off.

Ugh, could she look any more thrilled?

He nodded. "Yes, been single for quite a few years now, in fact."

"Being a single parent is difficult with normal hours," she replied quickly. "I could only imagine what you're going through, with such crazy ones."

"It's not too bad. It's just Celeste, and she's... fairly manageable. You... *you* have twins. That must be quite a handful."

"Not really. They're pretty good kids."

He smiled. "Good, then they won't have to see much of me."

Mom burst out laughing as if he'd said *the* funniest thing she'd ever heard.

"Oh, hell, I'm just kidding. Most of the other kids around here are pretty well-behaved, as well."

"Good, then I can relax when these two start meeting other kids in town and go out at night."

He tilted his head and leaned forward. "I wouldn't go that far. They *are* still teenagers".

"So very true," she sighed. "Well, thanks for making it out here so quickly. We were all pretty shaken up."

His lips thinned. "I'm sure. What a horrible experience for your first night in Shore Lake, too. I'm sorry you had to go through this."

"So are we," she said, frowning. "It was certainly an eventful evening. Crazy, huh?"

"I'd say." He put his hat on. "I'd better get going. I hope the next time we meet it's under much better circumstances."

My mom followed him to the door. "Me, too. Goodnight, Sheriff."

"Caleb," he said softly, looking down at her.

Her cheeks turned pink. "Goodnight, Caleb."

It was actually early morning but mom and Caleb didn't seem to notice. They were too busy staring at each other with their lonely middle-aged hormones.

"Goodbye, Sheriff," called Nathan from the couch with a shit-eating grin. Like me, he'd been studying them quietly, and from the look on his face, he also knew they were into each other.

"Yeah, see you," I added with a wave, hoping he'd just *leave,* already.

Caleb smiled once more with his gleaming white teeth and then *finally* walked out the front door.

"He's such a nice man," said mom, looking into space with a stupid grin. "It's so refreshing to know this town has a great guy like him patrolling the streets."

"Oh, you hardly know him," I snapped, getting off of the sofa. "He might not really be that nice. It could be an act."

Both my mom and brother stared at me in surprise.

I raised my chin. "Sorry, but it's true."

She shook her head. "Oh for Heaven's sake, Nikki, don't be so quick to judge other people."

I started walking up the steps to my bedroom, ready to fall into that soft pillow-top. "Whatever, I'm going to bed."

"She's just being a crab-ass," said Nathan.

"I heard that!" I hollered.

I knew it was true, though. It had been a long day and I was ready to sleep for the next two.

Chapter Four

I slept until almost eleven the next morning. Mom was already up, drinking coffee and working on her computer, when I padded downstairs in my bare feet.

"Morning," I said, pouring some coffee for myself. Normally, I wasn't a coffee drinker, but I really needed something stronger than orange juice to perk me up. Especially after the last few hours.

"Good morning," beamed my mother, who was always a morning person no matter how late she stayed up.

"Where's Nathan?"

"He's outside by the boat. We were thinking about taking it out on the lake within the hour."

I yawned. "I'll eat something and get ready."

"Good."

I took a drink of coffee and walked over to a large window facing the lake. The skies were blue and it looked like a beautiful day. Then I thought about the dead girl from last night.

"Um, did you really actually find her in the lake?" I asked. The idea of swimming in the lake when there'd been a floating body in it the night before was harrowing. I seriously doubted that I could even put my foot in the water.

"Why?"

I could tell from her expression that she knew where this was going.

I shrugged. "It's just kind of gross to think about swimming in it."

My brother entered the kitchen. "Don't worry, Nikki, that lake is so freaken big, I'm sure there are plenty of other bodies lost somewhere beneath the surface. People still swim in it all the time."

I shot him a dirty look. "That's gross."

Mom groaned. "Thanks, Nathan. Listen, people drown and it's just a fact of life. I'm sure every lake has stories of people disappearing in it, including the ones *you've* swam in the past."

I walked towards the doorway with my coffee. "That doesn't make it sound any more enticing. I think I'll just enjoy the view on the lake and try not to think about what's *under* it."

"Just make sure you're ready to go in an hour!" hollered Nathan as I stepped out of the kitchen. "Or we're leaving you behind."

~~~

An hour-and-a-half later, I'd changed into my new orange and pink bikini, and we were racing across the lake in a twenty-five-foot Stingray. Nathan was grinning from ear to ear, my mom was also smiling and desperately trying to hold her straw sunhat onto her head, but I was still thinking about the girl in the lake. I just couldn't shake the horror of knowing there'd been a body near the cabin we were now staying. I had to admit, the fact that my mother and brother were able to push it aside was a little disconcerting, too. It was almost like they'd forgotten all about it.

"This is great!" yelled Nathan over the motor as his light brown hair whipped in the wind. "There's hardly anyone out here and we have the entire lake to ourselves!"

It was true, but it was also early in the week. From the look of all the boats docked near the shoreline, this place was pretty busy on the weekends.

Nathan slowed down after crossing the entire lake and set the anchor. "Okay, I'm going for a swim," he said, smiling eagerly.

"Sounds good," said mom as she pulled out a book from her tote. "You know what I'm going to do – read and work on my tan."

I handed her some sunscreen. "Not without this. You'll be a lobster tonight as it is."

She smiled and began rubbing some of the coconut scented lotion into her skin.

"Coming in, twerp?" asked Nathan, removing his bright red T-shirt.

"Quit calling me that," I snarled. "Maybe later I'll come in and drown *you*."

He dove into the dark water. When he surfaced, he yelled, "Wow, it's really nice! Come on out, Nikki. Don't be such a wimp!"

The sun was shining, it was already eighty degrees and as I stared at him in the water, I had to admit, it did look *very* enticing.

I let out a long sigh and stood up. I lifted the white beach dress over my head and dove into the cool water.

"See," said Nathan when I popped my head back out. "It's not so bad."

I wiped some water away from my eyes and smiled. "Yeah, I guess not." It also didn't hurt that we were on the other side of the lake from where the girl had been found. For some reason, that comforted me quite a bit.

A small fishing boat was trolling towards us and I strained to see who was driving it, half expecting the sheriff who'd been making eyes at my mom earlier. Even today in her bikini, she'd caught the attention of a couple fishermen we'd passed by on the lake. Heck, I couldn't deny the fact that she looked pretty fit for someone reaching forty.

"Hey," shouted Nathan at the young man who stopped his boat next to ours. "How's it going?"

The dark-haired guy looked about our age, maybe a little older. He was wearing black sunglasses and blue-and-white striped swim trunks. "Pretty good. Nice boat!" he hollered back.

Nathan smiled. "It's not ours, but thanks."

The stranger removed his sunglasses and returned the smile. "I'm Duncan. You guys vacationing out here?"

"No," answered mom. "We're renting a cabin on the other side of the lake."

He nodded. "There are more than enough cabins available on this lake, that's for sure."

"Really? Why is that?" I asked.

He stared at me for a minute and then said, "I just meant that some of these cabins are only seasonal homes, so many of the owners rent them out during the year when they're not in use."

"Oh," I replied.

"I'm Anne, but the way," said mom. "And those two in the water are Nikki and Nathan."

"Nice meeting you all."

"You too," replied Nathan.

"Do you live on the lake then, Duncan?" she asked.

He nodded. "I live with my dad on the north side of the lake. He owns the boat repair shop over there, and our place is right next to it."

"Cool," said Nathan. "I suppose you get to see a lot of nice boats coming through there."

"Definitely, my dad's is the only repair shop nearby, so he's pretty busy, even with my help. Because the lake is so big and there's money on it, we definitely get some nice little yachts coming in for repairs."

I swam back over to our boat and climbed up the steps while Nathan and Duncan continued talking boats. As mom handed me a towel, I noticed Duncan stealing glances my way. When our eyes suddenly met, he quickly looked away.

"So, what do you guys do for fun here, other than fishing?" asked Nathan.

Duncan cleared his throat. "Actually, the town is having their annual end of summer barbeque this weekend at Turtle Beach. It's on the northern side of the lake, too. I'm sure they'll have tons of food and games. Then, at night they'll launch the fireworks. They do it every year."

"We'd better not miss that shindig," smiled my mom.

He nodded. "It's a pretty big deal. Almost everyone in town will be there."

"Will you be there?" I blurted out unexpectedly. I surprised everyone, even myself.

Duncan stared at me for a moment and smiled. "I wasn't planning on it, but it's starting to sound more interesting."

I could feel my face burning and it wasn't from the sun. "I, um... I just think it would be nice for Nathan to have someone to hang out with. He gets so bored, sometimes… "

"She's right," replied Nathan, grinning widely at me, as if he knew I was back-peddling. "I need a friend. I'm just so bored out of my mind now that we're in a new town and I have no friends to raise hell with."

He laughed. "I don't know much about raising hell, but if you're bored, you should stop by the shop later today. We just took in this mint Bluewater yacht that is *incredible*. I might even know someone with the keys who could give you a private tour."

"Sweet! I might have to take you up on that," said Nathan, his face brightening.

Just then, a couple flew by us on a pair of jet-skis and Duncan turned to watch them, giving me another opportunity to check him out. I had to admit that he was not only cute, but had nicely-sculpted pecs and arms. It was obvious that he worked his muscles when he wasn't working on boats. Before I had a chance to look away he turned back around and caught me staring. I immediately looked away, hoping my face wasn't as red as Nathan's trunks.

"What's wrong, Nikki?" asked mom, an amused expression on her face. "You feeling a little flushed?"

"No," I answered, a little too sharply.

"Oh. Okay."

"Your face *is* a little red," said Nathan, pointing to his cheek. He grinned. "Better use some sunscreen."

I shot him an angry look and he turned away, chuckling.

"I suppose I should get back to the marina. By the way, you ladies are invited, too, of course," said Duncan.

I looked up. "Okay."

"Thanks," said mom, "but maybe another time. I have too much to do this afternoon."

"No problem. I'll be around the shop all evening. Hope to see you there," said Duncan, his eyes drifting back to me again. Then he started the engine and was gone.

"That's cool," said Nathan as he got back on the boat after Duncan left. "Now I can check out some nice boats while Nikki checks out Duncan."

"Very funny."

He smiled. "Come on, I saw the way you were drooling over him!"

"I was not!" I retorted, scowling at him. "I was just checking his boat out."

He threw his head back and laughed. "Right! Since when do you have an interest in boats?"

"I always have."

My mom smiled and added her two cents. "Actually, I also noticed that you were checking out more than the boat."

"Whatever. You guys are seeing things. Anyway, you both should talk, what, about that redhead in the parking lot yesterday, and... Sheriff White Strips?"

My mom looked confused. "Sheriff *White Strips?*"

Nathan nodded. "Yeah, Caleb. His teeth were whiter than your pasty skin, mom. Bleached white."

She snorted. "You're funny."

"Sorry, couldn't resist," replied Nathan as he started the engine. He grabbed his bottle of water and took a swig. "I say we go back to the cabin now, I'm starving."

"Sounds good," she replied. "I've got plenty to do."

Nathan set his water in the cup-holder, turned on the engine, and we started back across the lake. A few seconds later, he grinned like a little kid and told us to hold on.

I grabbed the handle next to my seat right as he punched it down and we took off across the lake. I squealed in delight as we sped over the calm waters, the wind practically blowing my hair dry as we flew. Soon, we were near our neck of the woods and I pulled my beach-dress back over my bathing suit. As we slowed down, I noticed a middle-aged woman sitting on her dock, fishing. She smiled and raised her hand in greeting.

"Must be our neighbor," said mom, waving back. "Ernie mentioned that she was recently widowed. I think he said her name was Abigail. Very nice woman, I guess. Maybe it would be a good idea if I stopped by later and said hello."

I stared at the woman and nodded. "I would. She's probably sad and lonely."

She nodded. "I'm sure."

Nathan docked the boat near the end of the dock and we helped him secure it to the posts.

"That should be good enough for now," he said, testing the ropes. "I'll leave it out here in case we want to take it out again, later."

I stood up and looked down into the brown water. "So, um, it must be pretty deep, right here."

"Yeah," replied Nathan, grabbing his shirt from the boat. "That's why they built the dock this distance from the shore. It's safer for the boat if the lake ever gets low."

The water was so murky looking and I wondered if there were any more dead bodies below. I imagined someone's dead eyes staring up at me from below the surface and started to feel sick to my stomach.

"I'll meet you guys on shore," I said, getting up quickly.

"Are you okay?" called my mom.

"Just a little too much sun," I shouted back as I raced towards the cabin, feeling dizzy and anxious. As I passed the area where the body was found, I averted my eyes and tried not to panic any worse than I already was. When I made it to the cabin's porch, I closed my eyes and took a couple deep breaths.

"Hey," said my brother as he climbed the steps a minute later.

I smiled weakly.

He stared at me with concern. "You're really freaked out about that girl, aren't you?"

"Well, yeah. Aren't you?"

He sighed. "I'm trying to forget about it. She made a huge mistake when she started drinking that night, and hopefully her friends have learned from it. But I'm not going to dwell on it, and neither should you. Heck, you didn't even see the girl, I discovered her. I should be the one freaking out about it."

I nodded. "I know. It's just so... creepy."

He put an arm around my shoulder. "It is, but you have to let it go. Or mom will send you to a shrink, which, actually, she should have done a long time ago."

I pushed him away. "Ha-ha."

She met us on the porch and took out her keys. "Whew, it's getting hot out here. Thank goodness for air conditioning."

"Summer's almost over, mom. Then you'll be complaining about the cold. In fact, I've read that it gets *very* cold here," I said.

"That's when the fireplace will come in handy," she replied.

Nathan put the boat keys on one of the end tables. "Nikki, go get dressed and we'll drive into town to check it out. I need to start looking for a job, too."

"Okay," I replied. I'd worked at a boutique back home and my savings was starting to dwindle. I wanted my own car soon so I didn't have to rely on Nathan all the time.

"Then we'll go check out your boyfriend's boat repair shop," he said with a smirk.

"You're just full of jokes today."

Just then, mom, who'd been checking her voicemail, started smiling. She hung up the phone and stared at us. "Guess who asked me to dinner?"

I groaned. "Sheriff Snaggletooth?"

She frowned. "That's not fair, Nikki. Like I said before, he seems like a very nice man."

"You going for it?" asked Nathan, with a shit-eating grin.

She tapped her fingers on the banister. "Oh, I don't know. I'm not looking for anything right now, obviously, but it never hurts to get in good with a town's sheriff. Maybe I'll just invite him over to our house tonight for dinner. Can you pick up a couple of steaks in town, Nathan?"

He nodded. "But if you want wine, you'll have to get *that* yourself."

45

She snorted. "That's the last thing I need, to get tipsy in front of the town's sheriff."

Nathan smiled wickedly. "It might be fun. He can handcuff you if you get too out of hand."

Her eyes lit up. "Oh, I never thought of that."

"You're sick," I said, climbing the staircase. "Both of you."

"Oh, Nikki, I can't wait until the love bug nips you in the butt. I am going to tease the crap out of you," she said.

"Don't hold your breath. That's not happening anytime soon," I said.

"We'll see," she said.

"Be ready in thirty minutes, twerp," called Nathan. "We'll go cruising."

Chapter Five

I took a quick shower and changed into a dark blue halter sundress and white sandals. I pulled my hair into a loose up-do and applied a smidgeon of lip gloss.

"You look pretty," smiled mom as I entered the kitchen, looking for Nathan.

I looked down at my dress and shrugged. "Oh, it was one of the few things already unpacked."

She gave me a knowing smile and kissed the top of my head. "Don't break too many hearts in town."

"Ha-ha, mom. Very funny," I said, although I did feel sort of pretty in the new dress. It also wouldn't hurt to make a good impression on any kids who were hanging out in town.

Nathan was polishing up his Mustang when I found him outside. The red paint gleamed in the sun when he was finished.

"Now I'll definitely be a chic magnet," he teased, flexing his muscles. "Don't take offense if I ask you to duck down when the *ladies* are scoping me out."

I rolled my eyes. "Right."

"You'll see."

I got into the car and we took our time driving back into town.

"Hear from Deanna yet today?" I asked.

He grimaced. "Yeah. She called freaking out, again. I just don't know what to do about her. I mean, the more I think about it, the more I realize that I'm tired of the drama. Then I look at this town we've moved to and I think about all of the possibilities."

I smiled. "You mean all of the chicks?"

"Hell yeah," he laughed.

I shook my head at my brother, who was so predictable.

"Okay, keep your eyes peeled for something interesting," said Nathan, brushing his bangs away from his eyes. "Both of us need jobs."

As we entered the town I pointed right away to a diner called 'Ruth's.' "Let's stop in there and see if they're hiring."

"Good idea. I'm hungry again, anyway."

We were seated by a frazzled-looking waitress who appeared to be one of only two working. It was only three in the afternoon, but the place was packed.

"You wouldn't be hiring, would you?" I asked the other waitress, Amy, a blond with light blue eyes and an easy smile.

"Actually, funny you should ask, we're hiring for the nightshift," she said. "We're always hiring for that shift, so I guess it really isn't funny."

"That's fine. I'm desperately broke and need a job. Could you please get me an application?" I asked. "Oh, and," I handed her back the menu. "A Caesar salad?" I pointed to Nathan. "He's buying."

She laughed. "Okay, so anything to drink?"

"Just water," I replied.

"How are the burgers here, Amy?" asked Nathan.

"Oh, they're very good. That's why this place is always so busy. That and the fact that we're the only diner open twenty-four hours."

He smiled. "I'll take your word for it, then. I'd like a bacon double cheeseburger, an order of onion rings, and a chocolate milkshake."

She smiled back. "Hope you're hungry because they serve big portions here."

That's when Nathan turned on the charm. He leaned forward and smiled. "You know what... I already like this place, sis. Nice portions and even nicer waitresses. What more could a guy ask for?"

Amy blushed. She *was* very pretty and I'm sure that guys were always coming on to her, but even I had to admit, Nathan was a good-looking guy himself. Obviously, he knew it, too.

"I'll be back with your malt and water in just a moment," she said softly before she walked away.

"I guess Deanna is beginning to fade from your memory as the day progresses," I mused.

His face became serious. "Not really. I mean, there will always be a special place in my heart for her, but, I've decided to keep my options open. Heck, I'm young and shouldn't be tying myself down to one girl; especially one who's a few hundred miles away."

I folded my hands and nodded. "That's why I'm not going to waste time pining for any of the guys in town. After high school there will be college, and I don't want anything holding me back."

Amy returned with his milkshake and handed me an application.

"Um, if I were you I'd only request hours during the day or early evening."

"Why?" I asked, puzzled.

49

She looked around nervously and then whispered, "It's too dangerous around here at night."

Nathan raised his eyebrows. "What do you mean by dangerous?"

"Amy!" hollered someone behind the counter, who looked like the cook. "Order's up! They're waiting!"

"Sorry, I can't talk about it now," she mumbled. "Just take my word for it."

Then she left us both staring at each other in surprise.

I bit the side of my lower lip. "Wow, first a dead body in the lake and now this creepy warning?"

He waved his hand. "Oh, it might be nothing. Maybe she's talking about drunk drivers or something."

"I don't know, but, I'll take her word for it. I'd prefer to work during the day, anyway."

I finished the application just as our food arrived.

"I can take this and give it to the owner if you'd like. She'll be in later this evening," said Amy.

"Thanks," I said. "So, what did you mean earlier about it being dangerous around here at night?"

Her eyes darted around the restaurant again and I had this feeling like she was genuinely scared. Finally she cleared her throat and mumbled. "I didn't mean anything by it. Just forget I said anything."

At that moment I noticed that the diner was unusually quiet and I had the impression that some of the other customers were listening to our conversation. I decided it would be best just to drop the subject.

I raised my voice. "Oh. Well, yeah, if you could give the application to whoever does the hiring, I'd really appreciate it."

She nodded and then stepped away. I immediately noticed that the volume of the diner rose again and I stared at Nathan curiously.

"Okay, kind of weird," he said, under his breath. "Must be a small town thing?"

"Must be," I said, picking up my fork.

We finished our food and Nathan left a big tip for Amy, who was so busy she could barely make it back to the table, to refill our glasses.

"You dropped something," called Amy as we were leaving the diner. Before I could respond, she handed me a folded-up note and hurried away.

"What was that all about?" asked Nathan as we walked to the car."

The sun was bright and I put my shades on. "Don't know. We'll read it in the car."

When we got into the Mustang, I immediately opened the note and read it out loud. "Lock your doors at night and don't invite any strangers inside." A shiver ran up my spine and I turned to Nathan. "Okay, that's really freaky."

Nathan's cell phone began to ring before he could respond. "It's mom," he said, answering it.

I could hear them talking about her date with the sheriff and then he hung up.

"I guess it's going to be a late dinner, so we don't have to be home for a few hours. The sheriff is working a little later and isn't getting off until sometime after nine."

I snorted. "If it's dangerous here at night, it would make sense that he's really busy."

"Listen," said Nathan, as we pulled out of the parking lot. "I wouldn't go blowing everything out of proportion. It's possible that Amy was friends with that dead girl and doesn't trust anyone right now. Or maybe, she's a little crazy."

I sighed. "Or maybe, she's just worried about us. You have to admit that finding a dead body practically at our doorstep isn't the best housewarming gift."

"Since the sheriff is coming to dinner tonight, why don't we just ask him about it? He'd certainly know if there was something wicked happening around here after dark."

"Maybe," I mumbled.

"Hey, that must be Duncan's dad's shop," said Nathan, slowing the car down.

I looked up and noticed a large boat marina with a big sign that read: "Sonny's Boat Repairs." Nathan pulled into the parking lot and we both got out.

"Wow, check out all of those boats," pointed Nathan, his face lighting up. "Oh man, I think I just had an orgasm."

I glared at him. "God, you are so disgusting."

There was a fenced-in storage area for some of the smaller boats not docked at the marina. On the other side was the repair shop.

"I'd like to get myself an old Carver after I find a job," said Nathan as we walked towards the shop's entrance. "I hear you can get one relatively inexpensive and fix it up."

Nathan and my dad have always loved boats. In fact, we used to own a twenty-four foot Bayliner before my parents split up. Then dad had to sell the boat and Nathan's been pining for his own ever since.

"Hey!" called Duncan, coming towards us. "You made it."

"Yeah," said Nathan. "Now that we're here, I have to admit, I'm jealous. You're surrounded by some pretty amazing boats."

Duncan started telling us about another high-end yacht that needed repairs. I have to admit, though, I was paying more attention to him than what he was saying. Up close, he appeared much taller than I'd remembered and had a contagious smile. His eyes were a silvery gray color, and every time he glanced my way, I felt my cheeks heat up.

"I just realized something," he said. "You're twins, aren't you?"

"Yeah," said Nathan, putting his arm around my shoulders. "She's the ugly one, poor little thing."

My jaw dropped and I smacked him in the shoulder for what had to be the tenth time that day. "You are such a shit."

"But I'm the good-looking one," he laughed.

Duncan shook his head and stared at us in amusement. "Sorry, dude, but I think you might have that wrong. Nikki here seems to have absorbed all the beauty genes, leaving you with a great sense of humor, though."

"Oh, yeah," I laughed, secretly thrilled that Duncan thought I was cute, "and even his sense of humor leaves a lot to be desired."

Nathan pouted. "And I thought you invited me along because I was the cuter twin."

"No, but I have to say, you still have a nice butt," joked Duncan.

"Pilates," said Nathan, turning around to show us.

"Okay, enough!" I interrupted. "Now I've realized that you are both a couple of dorks."

"From one dork to another," said Nathan. "I'm ready to see some yachts. Lead the way, you sexy thang."

Duncan burst out laughing and turned around to lead us towards the marina. I quickly checked out his rear and decided that he definitely didn't need any Pilates.

Chapter Six

An hour later, after getting a few secret tours on some of the largest yachts I'd ever seen, we followed Duncan into the main shop to meet his dad, Sonny.

"Hello," said Sonny, who was an older version of Duncan, minus the hair, "nice to meet the both of you."

Nathan held out his hand and shook Sonny's. "Thanks for letting Duncan give us a glimpse of some of these sweet yachts," he said. "You must be extremely busy with all of those boats out there."

"Tell me about it," said Sonny. "I can barely keep up. I'm going to have to hire someone to help around the shop, especially now that fall is just around the corner. Many of these boats need to be winterized, and soon."

I looked at Nathan, who was already way ahead of me.

"What kind of experience do you need? I'm looking for a job," said my brother.

Sonny rubbed his bald head. "I can't imagine you'd know how to repair boat engines at your age, although Duncan does, but that's because he's been around them most his life. You know, I could still use someone to take care of the customers, order parts, and do some of the lighter maintenance. That would free up a lot of time for me and my son."

I could see that Nathan was getting really excited. "Listen," he said, his eyes sparkling. "I'm your man. I'm a very hard worker and learn quickly."

Sonny leaned back in his chair. "Okay. We'll have you fill out an application and I'll certainly consider you. I do have a couple mechanics who work the graveyard shift, so what I could really use is someone who doesn't mind doing a little grunt work."

"Grunt is my middle name," smiled Nathan.

Sonny smiled. "That's what I like to hear."

While Nathan started filling out the application, Duncan asked me if I wanted anything to drink.

"Um, sure... water?"

"Come on, I'll show you our luxurious break room."

I followed Duncan to the back of the shop and we entered into a small room with pop and snack machines.

"Here," he said, handing me a bottle of water from the back of the fridge. "I'll give you one from my secret stash. If I don't hide them, they seem to disappear overnight."

I laughed. "Really? Thanks."

"So," he said as he sat down and stretched out his long legs. "How do you like Shore Lake so far?"

"Seriously, it's kind of a hard question to answer. Last night we found a body near the lake, and today, one of the waitresses at Ruth's passed me a note that warned us to stay inside after dark and not invite any strangers inside."

His eyes widened. "Seriously?! Are you kidding me?"

I took a sip of the water. "No, I wish I was." I set my water down and pulled out the note Amy had given me.

He read it and frowned. "Very strange. So, do the cops know whose body you found?"

"Some girl around my age, Tina Johnson?"

He scratched his head. "Tina Johnson? To tell you the truth, I don't really know many of the locals. I only stay with my dad during the summer and then for the rest of the year, I live with my mom in Minnesota."

"Oh, so you're going back to Minnesota next month when school starts?"

He smiled. "I graduated last spring, so now I can stay wherever I want."

"What are you going to do now?" I asked.

He sighed. "Probably help my dad out while I take some engineering classes at the local college."

"What about your mom?"

"She just remarried and is pretty busy with her new husband," he said. "My dad doesn't really have anyone else but me, so I'm probably sticking around here."

I took a sip of water and set it down. "Well, it sounds like your dad really needs you in more ways than one."

He nodded. "What about your old man?" he asked and then looked embarrassed. "I'm sorry, I probably shouldn't have asked. If he's passed away or something, I apologize for my lack of tactfulness."

I smiled humorlessly. "Actually, there are times that I wish he *had* passed away. I know that sounds really cold, but he's an asshole. Thank goodness my mom is no longer with him."

"Then cheers to that," he said, tapping my water bottle with his.

"Cheers."

He re-capped his water. "So, you mentioned the dead girl, do they think she was murdered?"

"No, it sounds like she liked to party a little too much and may have accidently killed herself."

"What about the waitress at the diner?" he asked, biting his lower lip. "That was a pretty weird."

"Very." I sat back in the chair. "So, um, have you heard anything about missing people or other bodies being discovered near the lake?"

He looked thoughtful. "No, not really; although, there have been plenty of people moving recently. That's why I mentioned the cabins. Either people are selling or just renting out their lake homes."

"Hey, Nikki," said Nathan as he stepped into the break room, "are you ready to get going? I want to pick up those steaks for mom before it gets too late."

I looked at my watch and noticed it was already after seven. "Yeah, we'd better leave."

"Thanks for stopping by, guys," said Duncan, standing up. He lowered his voice. "I'll work on my dad so he'll hire you."

Nathan laughed. "Sounds good. I'll give you a call in a couple of days if I don't hear from him, to see what's going on. If anything, we can go cruising."

"Definitely. And don't forget about the barbeque this weekend," said Duncan. "Now that Nikki's practically begged me to be your date, Nathan."

Nathan's eyes widened innocently. "Oh, what ever will I wear?" he asked, standing kind of prissy. "Do you like pink, Duncan?"

Duncan looked at my dress and then winked. "Actually, I prefer blue."

Chapter Seven

It was dark by the time we made it home and mom was on the deck, desperately trying to figure out the grill.

"Step aside before you blow us all up," ordered Nathan, handing her the package of steaks.

"No arguments here," she answered. "I prefer cooking on the stove myself, but the steaks taste so much better on the grill. Thanks for picking them up, by the way."

"No problem. Just don't give the sheriff mine, it's the thirty-ouncer," he replied.

"Of course not, you bottomless pit," she said. "But we're also having potatoes, pasta salad, and corn on the cob. So pace yourself tonight, if you can."

He snorted. "That's it? No dessert?"

"Cheesecake," she said. "But let's make sure our guest gets a piece before you get your mitts on it."

"You should have made two, and then you wouldn't have to worry about it," he joked.

She raised her finger. "I'm not going to worry about it because you're going to wait until everyone else has had a piece before you devour the rest."

"Okay, I can live with that."

"You look nice," I told her. She was wearing a lilac colored blouse and a new white skirt I'd never seen before.

"Thanks," she smiled. "So, how was your trip into town?"

"It started out a little strange but got better," I answered.

"What do you mean?"

Nathan interrupted. "Oh, she applied for a job at the local diner and some waitress slipped her a note with an ominous warning."

"What?"

I showed her the piece of paper and she shrugged. "That *is* pretty odd. Maybe she knew the deceased girl? Who knows, she may think there was foul play involved."

"Maybe there was," I said.

She frowned. "The sheriff didn't seem to think so. We'll ask him about it again when he gets here."

"Okay," I said, putting the note away. I didn't think he'd tell us much, however. Having a father for a cop taught me that they weren't keen on divulging information like that.

"So, did you guys make it to Duncan's boat shop?"

"Yeah," said Nathan. "And his dad is hiring for shop help, so I filled out an application."

Her eyes widened. "Wow, that means both of you might have jobs before the end of the summer? That's amazing!"

"Yeah, I know. I need money and a car, badly," I said.

"If you get a job, I'll help you find a car and you can pay me back in installments. But, don't expect anything fancy," she said.

"Seriously? Thanks, mom," I replied, throwing my arms around her. I'd never owned my own car before, although I had my license. I started thinking about all of the possibilities and became giddy.

"You bet. I know it's tough not having a car; especially, now that you'll be a senior."

As I pulled away, my eyes caught a movement in the woods. At first, I thought it was a deer or some other wild animal, but then in a blur, it shot up into the trees. I wasn't sure, but I could have sworn its eyes were glowing, too. Just like the so-called "Peeping Tom."

"Something's in the woods," I whispered hoarsely.

"What?" asked my mother.

Nathan stepped off the deck and began walking slowly towards the trees.

"What the hell are you doing?" barked mom.

He raised his hand. "Calm down. It's probably just a deer or something."

I pointed up towards the top of the trees. "It flew up there, and I doubt it was a reindeer."

My mom released a heavy sigh. "Then it was just a bird. Don't scare me like that."

I shook my head, vehemently. "No, it wasn't a bird."

Nathan walked back onto the deck. "Of course it was a bird. Or maybe a flying squirrel."

I put my hands on my waist. "It wasn't a small animal, okay? It was big! Bigger than you," I told him.

"The shadow probably looked a lot larger than the animal. When it's dark like this, your eyes can play tricks on you. Think about it, nothing my size would be able to fly up into a tree," he said. "It's not possible."

"I know what I saw," I snapped, glaring at him, "and it was big. I'm going into the cabin. This place is really starting to give me the creeps."

"It's been a long day," said my mom, as I opened the patio door. "Caleb should be here in another hour. If you're

60

hungry, Nikki, eat some of that pasta salad I made. It's in the refrigerator. Oh, and put these steaks in there too, will you?"

She handed them to me and my stomach started rumbling as I went into the kitchen. Although I was still freaked out about the flying shadow, I was also starving, as I hadn't eaten anything since my salad at the diner earlier.

I opened up the refrigerator and took out the large bowl of pasta, setting it on the counter. As I began scooping out some of the salad, the hair on the back of my neck stood straight up. I raised my eyes to the window facing me and let out a bloodcurdling scream. A pale face was staring at me through the glass. It disappeared quickly and I leaped away from the window in terror.

"What's wrong?" hollered my brother, rushing into the kitchen.

"Someone was watching me," I choked, pointing towards the window. "Through there!"

He stared at my frightened face then grabbed a butcher knife from the block.

"What are you planning on doing with that?" cried mom, entering the kitchen.

"Nikki thinks there's someone out there." He raised the knife. "If there *is* someone, I'm not going unarmed."

Just then the doorbell rang, startling us all.

"I'll get it," said mom. "Hopefully it's the sheriff and he can take a look around outside."

We followed her to the front door and she swung it open.

"Hello," smiled Caleb, holding out two bottles of wine, a red and a white. "I wasn't sure if you were a wine drinker or not. I brought red and white, just in case."

"Thank God you're here," she said, grabbing a bottle of wine and pulling him through the door. "Nikki thinks someone is lurking around outside."

"Think?" I snapped. "I know there is. Someone was in the woods watching all of us, and then a face stared at me through the window."

Caleb was dressed in civilian clothing, jeans and a white polo shirt, but he reached down by his ankle and pulled out a gun. "Okay, I'll go take a look. You guys stay inside and lock your doors."

"Mom, I'm seriously really scared," I said, as she locked the door. "What the hell is going on around here?"

She walked over and hugged me. "Don't worry, it'll be fine."

"What if it's dad?" said Nathan, his face pale. "What if he's found us and is trying to scare the shit out of us?"

"Oh, hell, I never even considered that," said mom, looking quite troubled, herself. "I hope not."

"Would he do that?" I asked.

She shrugged. "I don't know. The law is after him now. He might do anything. I can't imagine how he found out where we were staying, though. The only person who knew was Ernie."

"I think you should call Ernie and make sure he's okay," said Nathan.

She moved towards the phone, her face white. "I'll call him right now."

There was a loud knock at the door. "It's me. Let me in. Everything's okay," called Caleb.

Mom put down the phone and rushed to the door. "Did you find anything?" she asked, when he stepped inside.

He smiled. "Actually, I found a couple of raccoons outside that were looking pretty mischievous. I didn't find anything else out of the ordinary, though."

"Um, did you see footprints by any of the kitchen windows, or any prints?" asked Nathan.

He bit back a smile. "I didn't see much, I'm sorry. But I really don't think there's anyone out there."

"I know what I saw, and it was a human face, staring at me through the kitchen window," I said. "It freaked the crap out of me."

His eyebrows shot up. "Okay, what did this person look like?"

I sighed. "It was hard to tell, it happened so fast."

"If you couldn't really tell, then it's quite possible that you saw an animal," said Caleb, walking towards the window. He lifted one of the blinds and peered outside. "There are a lot of those in these woods."

"It moved so quickly, I couldn't tell if it was a man or woman, but it definitely wasn't an animal. I'm sure of that," I said

He released the blind and walked back over to us. "I can look around again, if it makes you feel better."

"Thank you, Caleb," interrupted my mom. "This family has been through so much that it would really be comforting if you could do that for us."

He nodded slowly. "Okay, I understand. I'll be back in a few minutes."

"Thank you," I said, as he walked back towards the door.

"No problem. If it's going to calm everyone down, I'll be happy to do it."

"I told you he was a nice man," said mom after he left the cabin again.

Even I had to admit, it was almost comforting having him around. Almost.

Caleb took much longer this time, but when he returned, he still hadn't discovered anything unusual.

"Thank you for doing that, Caleb," said my mother, handing him a glass of red wine. "You could probably use a little of this right now."

"I thought you'd never ask," he answered with a lopsided grin. "Although I'd better not overindulge; I hear the cops in this area are pretty wicked."

She giggled and then turned to Nathan. "Honey, can you fire up the grill? I'm sure everyone is starving by now."

"Yeah, I'm fading away," said Nathan, raising his hands in front of his face. "I can barely see my hands."

Mom smiled and shook her head. Then she turned to me. "Nikki? Honey, why don't you go upstairs and rest for a little while. I'll fix you a plate of food and bring it up later, if you don't feel like coming back down."

I glanced at Caleb, who was staring at my mother like she was a filet mignon. I knew right then that it was time to make an exit.

"Okay, I need to change anyway," I said, getting off the couch. As I left, I could hear them talking and wanted to puke at the way she was flirting with the sheriff. It wasn't that I didn't like Caleb; I just didn't think she was ready to start anything after what just happened.

I raced upstairs to my bedroom, still feeling tense. The gnawing feeling of dread in the pit of my stomach was driving me crazy and I just wanted to go back to my old home in San Diego.

Feeling helpless, I kept the lights off and changed into a pair of shorts and a T-shirt, keeping my attention on the balcony window. When I finished, I grabbed my bat and slowly walked over to the glass and worked up the nerve to look down below. I half expected to see some kind of ghoul lurking around in the darkness. Nothing appeared out of the ordinary, however, which still wasn't enough to calm my nerves.

"What are you doing?" whispered Nathan next to my ear.

"Holy crap! Don't you ever freak me out like that again!" I snapped. "You almost gave me a fucking heart attack!"

"Wow, I'm sorry. Just settle down, will you?"

I rubbed the beads of sweat from my forehead and then looked at him. "I don't care what the sheriff says, I saw someone out there watching me in the kitchen."

He sighed. "I'm not sure what you saw, either, but what I do know is that ever since we found that girl's body, you've been going crazy. I mean, isn't it possible that you saw a raccoon staring at you in the window? You said so yourself, you couldn't even see the face very well."

"I can tell the difference between a raccoon's face and a person's, Nathan. I'm not a complete moron," I said, glancing through the window again.

We both stared outside in silence for a while.

"Maybe it really is dad, then," he said softly. "He might be trying to frighten her or all of us."

"I don't know. It just doesn't feel right. Dad had major anger issues, but he doesn't seem the type of person who'd waste his time doing this kind of thing. In fact, he's probably hiding on the other side of the world by now with the help of some of his cop friends."

"Maybe," said Nathan.

I yawned. "I guess I'm going to bed. I lost my appetite anyway. Could you tell mom? I don't really want to go back down there. It's nauseating."

He chuckled. "Okay, Nik, if you need us, just holler."

"Oh, you'll hear me. Count on that."

After he left, I turned on the television and watched a movie about a girl who'd fallen in love with both a vampire and a werewolf. I'd already seen it a million times, so my eyelids grew heavy fairly quickly. Ten minutes later I was out cold in my bed and dreaming of Duncan, who turned into a werewolf and was trying to kill my own vampire boyfriend. Every time I tried to see the vampire's face, however, it was a blur.

Chapter Eight

Mom was still sleeping when I woke the next morning, which was pretty odd, considering it was after ten and she never usually slept past eight.

"Hey," I said to Nathan, who was eating a monstrous bowl of cereal and watching television at the kitchen counter.

He smirked. "It lives."

"Very funny, butthead," I answered.

"Just kidding, twerp," he replied with his mouth full. "Hey, guess who called for you this morning?"

Duncan? "Who?"

"The manager at that diner you put in an application for."

I stared at him in surprise. "Wow, really?"

"Yeah, you're supposed to call her back if you're still interested in setting up an interview. Here," he said, handing me a slip of paper, "call Rosie at that number."

"Awesome," I said, grinning from ear to ear.

Ten minutes later I had an interview set up for later that afternoon.

"Wow, that was fast," said Nathan. "I guess I'll have to give you a ride."

"Or, you could just loan me your car."

He snorted. "Right. Nobody drives that car but me. Not even Deanna got the privilege of driving my baby."

"Hi, kids," yawned mom as she shuffled into the kitchen.

"You were up late," said Nathan.

She turned on the Keurig and smiled. "Well, Caleb's an interesting man. He's traveled all over the world and we talked for hours about his crazy adventures."

"Small town sheriff-slash-traveler extraordinaire, huh?" smirked Nathan.

Her eyes lit up. "He's been to so many places, it's amazing."

"Oh, shoot," I said. "Speaking of Caleb, I forgot to tell him about the note I received from the waitress yesterday."

Mom waved her hand. "Oh, I mentioned it to him and he didn't seem too concerned. He said this town has had its share of crimes, but there certainly wasn't anything to be afraid of, even in the dark. He also mentioned that Amy was having a hard time getting over the loss of her friend, the one we found. It's made her a little… unstable."

I narrowed my eyes. "What do you mean, unstable?"

She sighed. "I'm not supposed to talk about this, but, she tried to commit suicide a couple weeks ago."

"Wow," replied Nathan. "That's rough."

Mom nodded. "I guess her parents have been trying frantically to get her help, even going as far as putting her on antidepressants, but obviously, she still has some emotional issues."

"And Caleb knows all about this?" I asked.

She poured some cream into her coffee. "Yeah, his daughter, Celeste went to school with Amy. They both graduated in June."

67

"Oh," I said.

"How did you sleep last night?" she asked me.

"Fine, although, I had some disturbing dreams. Other than that, I slept pretty well."

"Holy crap," interrupted Nathan. He turned up the volume on the television and I stared at it in horror. A picture of the waitress who'd served us yesterday flashed across the screen.

"Seventeen-year-old Amy Kreger was found in the woods near Lake Shore, early this morning," said the female reporter, standing next to an old Chevy Camaro. "Her car had been found abandoned by the side of the road with drug paraphernalia sitting openly on the front seat. When police officers were called to investigate, they found the deceased in the woods with self-inflicted wounds on both wrists. Tragically, this young girl was close friends with Tina Johnson, who went missing a few weeks ago. Tina's body was found just two days ago, washed up onshore in an undisclosed location. Police officials do not suspect foul play in either case."

Nathan turned off the television and we all stared at each other in shock.

I cleared my throat. "No foul play in either case? Seems unlikely now, doesn't it?

"Maybe it's just two very disturbed girls," replied Nathan.

Mom shook her head sadly. "That poor girl. Her parents must be devastated."

"She was so pretty, too," said Nathan. "It just goes to show that you can't judge people by what's on the outside. Amy must have been pretty messed up."

I stood up. "Did it ever occur to you that maybe she wasn't messed up?"

"Nikki…" said my mom.

"They found drugs in her car. Obviously, she had issues," said Nathan.

"Whatever, I'm going to lie down in my room for a while," I said. "This is nuts."

I went upstairs and took out the note Amy had given me. It gave me the chills to know that she was now dead.

"Hey," said Nathan from my doorway. "I'm taking the boat out in an hour if you want to get some fresh air and clear your head."

I nodded. "Yeah, that sounds like a good idea. Is mom coming?"

He shook his head. "No, she's going into town to talk with her new boss. I guess she's starting work on Monday."

"Okay. I'll be down in an hour."

He left and I took a quick shower, still thinking about Amy and the face in the window last night. I wasn't sure at this point which was more disturbing. I knew one thing, however; I was going to try and talk mom out of staying here. Something was going on in this town. I wasn't sure if it was just one crazy freak or a group of them. What I did know was that there were two dead girls and now someone was spying on us. At this point, dad seemed less frightening.

After I toweled off, I slipped on a pair of shorts and a tank top, then piled my hair on top of my head.

"Ready?" asked Nathan when I met him downstairs.

"Yeah, let me grab something to eat first"

When I entered the kitchen, mom was standing over the sink with the water running, her face pasty white.

"Are you okay?"

She nodded. "Yeah, I think I had a little too much wine last night. It's finally catching up to me."

"Really? A delayed hangover? That's weird. Hey, what's that on your neck?" I asked, staring at her skin. "Did you get bit by a couple of mosquitos?"

She touched her neck. "I must have."

The skin on her neck was definitely swollen and there were two small red bumps just below her ear.

I squinted. "Does it itch? It looks pretty inflamed."

My mom had always been very sensitive to bug bites, so it wasn't a surprise that her skin was tender and sore-looking.

She shrugged. "No, not really. It's a little tender, though."

"You should put something on that," I said, turning away from her. I reached into the cupboard and grabbed a box of chewy granola bars. "Some of that Neosporin stuff."

"I will." She touched her head and groaned. "God, remind me not to have more than one glass of wine the next time anyone offers."

I snorted. "No doubt."

She grabbed a paper towel, poured cool water over it, and then dabbed her forehead. "You know, I think I'm going to lie back down for a while."

"Hey," I said as she began walking away, "I have an interview this afternoon. That diner I was telling you about."

"Good job, sweetheart. I'm sure you'll get it."

I'm sure, too. They're really in need of help now that Amy's gone, I thought bitterly.

Thirty minutes later, Nathan and I were racing across the lake in the boat again.

"Let's head over to Sonny and Duncan's marina!" he yelled over the engine.

I gave him the thumbs-up. I had to admit, the thought of seeing Duncan again was stirring up the butterflies in my stomach.

The sun was already hot, and by the time we reached the marina, I could feel the back of my neck and shoulders begin to burn. I grabbed some sunscreen and started lathering it on.

"Hey!" called Duncan, who was putting gasoline into a fishing boat.

"What's up, Dunc?" asked Nathan.

He smiled. "Not much."

Nathan docked the boat and tied it. "So, did your dad mention anything about the job yet?"

Duncan laughed. "Haven't had time to talk about it. But I think you have the best shot so far. My dad seems to like you."

"Cool. Nikki already has an interview later this afternoon for a waitressing job."

Duncan looked at me. "Ruth's?"

"Yeah. By the way, did you watch the news this morning?"

He shook his head. "No, been working."

I told him about Amy and then mentioned the face in the window.

His eyebrow shot up. "Seriously? Wow, it's weird that you mentioned that, because I'm pretty sure that someone was watching me last night, too."

Chapter Nine

My stomach clenched up like a fist. "Really?"

He nodded. "It was just before midnight and I was in the kitchen, having a snack. I heard some weird scraping noises near one of the windows, and when I looked up, I could have sworn someone ducked away. I even went outside to check it out."

I shivered. "Did you find anyone?"

"I didn't. But I felt like someone was watching me when I was outside, too. I have to admit, it kind of scared the shit out of me."

I turned to Nathan. "So, do you think I'm still seeing things?"

He looked at both of us and shook his head. "Fine, I believe you. Maybe it's a Peeping Tom?"

Duncan shrugged. "Could be, or something worse. It also happened to me a few weeks ago, too, but I thought I was just imagining things. In fact, now that I think about it, I believe it happened around the night that girl went missing, Tina Johnson."

I looked at both of them. "And last night, Amy was murdered."

Nathan groaned. "Nikki, quit it already. You watched the news! They have evidence that she committed suicide. They found drugs in her car and her wrists were slashed. She was messed up. Caleb's daughter even told him she had issues."

"Maybe, but I still have a hard time believing it. Someone could have killed her and covered it up. She was terrified of something. Why would she warn us if she wasn't?"

Nathan walked over and shook me playfully. "You're making something out of nothing. Okay, even if someone was watching both of you last night, it's probably just some pervert."

"And that's supposed to make me feel better?" I asked incredulously.

With a determined look on his face, Duncan said, "You know what? I think we should try and catch whoever's doing it."

"How?" I asked, my heart beginning to race. It sounded frightening and exciting at the same time.

"We could set up video cameras. I have some extra ones in storage that we keep for the marina. Hey, we could monitor both our cabins."

I nodded, feeling the surge of adrenaline strike every part of my body. "I think we should! If we get it on camera, the sheriff will take us seriously!"

"Fine," replied Nathan. "If it's going to help you get over your paranoia, Nikki, I'll help Duncan set it up."

"Okay," said Duncan. "I'm pretty busy this morning, but around lunchtime, I can get them out of storage and start setting things up."

"I have to bring Nikki to her interview this afternoon. We'll stop by your place after and you can follow us out to the cabin to set up something there."

Duncan nodded. "Sounds good."

"Thanks, Duncan," I said softly. "I've been going nuts about this."

Duncan's eyes met mine. "You're welcome."

"We'd better get back," said Nathan, looking at his watch. "I'm hungry and Nikki probably wants to prepare for her interview."

His eyes lowered and he grinned. "If she keeps that outfit on, she'll definitely get hired."

My cheeks burned red. I didn't know what to say, although I had to admit, I was beyond delighted.

Nathan snickered. "Wow, Duncan, I've never seen Nikki at a loss for words. Do you want to move in with us? Could sure use the peace."

I flipped him the bird. "Very funny."

Nathan untied the boat and pushed us away from the dock. "See you later, Dunc."

"Yeah, see you," I said.

"Goodbye and good luck with your interview," he replied.

"Thanks."

As we drifted away and Nathan started the engine, I put my sunglasses on and watched as Duncan began fueling another boat. Not only was he cute, but he believed me, without question. So far, he was the only real good thing I'd encountered in Shore Lake.

Chapter Ten

Three hours later, I sat across from Rosie, who'd inherited Ruth's diner from her mother several years back. As she looked over my job application, I studied the rail-thin, bleach-blond woman and gathered she was somewhere in her sixties because of her weathered skin. She did have a cigarette resting behind her ear, so she could have actually been younger.

"You're new in town?" she asked in a gravelly voice.

"Yes, we just moved here a couple of days ago."

"Have you ever waitressed before?"

I sighed. "No. I worked at a boutique, though, so I've used a register before and have experience with customers."

She nodded. "You'll be on your feet a lot. Do you have any problems with that?"

I shook my head.

"Are you available to work nights?"

I bit the side of my lip. "I'd prefer days, if that's possible."

She studied me. "To be honest, I really need the help at night. I don't expect you to work past midnight, but my second shift is really hurting right now. I'm even willing to pay you an extra dollar an hour."

I sighed. "That's fine. Is there a chance that I can switch to days in the future? When school starts, my mom won't want me working past ten."

She nodded. "We won't make you work past nine during the week, but we'd need you until midnight on Friday or Saturday. Would that be an issue for you?"

"No," I answered.

She asked me a few more questions then hired me on the spot.

"Wow, that was fast," I blurted out.

She smiled. "We need the help, desperately. Can you start tomorrow?"

I nodded. "That shouldn't be a problem."

"You'll be training with Susan. So, we'll see you around four, tomorrow afternoon?"

I agreed and then she found me a uniform, which wasn't easy with my short frame. When it was all said and done, I left the diner so giddy that I wanted to scream.

"Let me guess, they hated you," smiled Nathan as I got into his Mustang. He'd been listening to the stereo and waiting for me in the parking lot.

I held up my hand. "I start tomorrow."

He slapped it. "Good job. I also have awesome news; Sonny called my cell phone and I start next Monday. Pending a drug test. I'm sure Duncan had everything to do with it, but I'm not complaining."

"That's great!" I said and then swore. "So, how are we going to work this out? I need a ride to and from work until I'm able to get a car. They want me working second shift."

"If I'm at the marina, I'll try and work something out with Sonny. Maybe I can take my lunch break and pick you up at the cabin? I'm sure he'll be cool with that. It'll just be for a little while, anyway."

I smiled. "Thanks. I know it isn't easy driving me around everywhere."

"Yeah, you're kind of a pain in the ass," he smirked.

I smacked him in the shoulder again. "You are an *ass* so I guess it kind of makes sense."

He rubbed his arm. "I must have a permanent bruise there from you beating up on me all the time. Show your brother some love," he pouted.

"Shut your yap and you won't get hurt."

"Ho, ho… big words from such a little twerp," he said.

I raised my fist again. "You don't listen very well, do you?"

He snorted and shook his head. "You're so violent."

I smiled. "Just remember that."

"So, let's head over to the marina and check out the surveillance equipment," he said.

"Okay."

Nathan gave me a sideways glance. "Although I'm sure Duncan will be monitoring someone else."

"What?"

Nathan smiled. "Oh, come on. You know he has the hots for you."

"Whatever," I said, looking out the window.

"He does, but that's okay because he seems like a decent guy. I think you should go for it."

I snorted. "Go for it? Look, I'm not interested in going for anything right now."

"Right. That's why you blush every time he looks your way."

"I do not!"

"You're face turns as red as a tomato."

I could feel it burning right now as he teased me.

"See!" he laughed.

"It's just a sunburn!"

He shook his head and gave me a knowing look.

I turned up the radio and tried avoiding his smartass grin.

When we arrived at the marina, we walked over to the cabin next door, where Duncan was adjusting his surveillance equipment.

"All set?" asked Nathan.

He nodded. "Yeah, I've got cameras set up all around the perimeter of this place. There's no way I'll miss this guy if he comes back."

"You still want to do our cabin, too?"

He nodded. "Yeah, I'll follow you in my truck. I'm ready whenever you are."

"Shoot, I just remembered, I have to pick up mom's dry cleaning. Is it okay if Nikki rides with you and shows you where we live? I'll meet you both at the cabin as soon as I'm done."

My eyes narrowed, I didn't remember her requesting anything like that. In fact, she was supposed to drive into town herself sometime today. I didn't mention any of this, however. I didn't want Duncan to think Nathan was trying to play matchmaker.

"Sure," replied Duncan. He looked at me. "Should we get going?"

I nodded and then followed him to a white pickup truck with "Sonny's Boat Repairs" on it.

Duncan apologized. "Sorry, it's nothing fancy but it gets me places."

I smiled. "It's better than what I have, which is nothing."

He turned the radio on and glanced at me. "You look nice. How did your interview go?"

I smiled. "I got the job. In fact, I start tomorrow evening."

"See, I told you, you'd get it."

I looked down at my clothes. For the interview, I had worn a peach silk blouse and mid-length black skirt with heels. My feet were already killing me.

"I guess I know where I'll be eating dinner from now on."

I laughed. "It's *your* stomach. I'm not cooking, you know, I'm only serving."

He shrugged. "That's okay. I'll come in and be one of those annoying customers who sits and drinks coffee all day long, but I'll leave a much better tip."

"As long as you tip, I'll save you a booth."

"So," he said, changing the subject. "Do you remember anything about the face you saw in the window?"

I shook my head. "No, it left so quickly. I know it wasn't an animal like the sheriff suggested."

"You called the sheriff?"

"He came over for dinner. He has the hots for my mom."

He laughed. "Boy, he works fast."

"My mom is already looking at engagement rings."

He raised his eyebrows.

I laughed. "I'm just kidding."

"I was going to say..."

"No, but she certainly likes him. Anyway, he went out and looked around for a while, but figured it was just a raccoon."

"But you don't believe it?"

"No," I said. "There wasn't any fur on the face that I saw."

I then explained about the feeling of being watched when we were on the deck and the shadow that flew into the trees. As I went on, his face darkened.

"What?" I asked.

79

"That's happened to me before, too. I thought I was imagining it and made excuses, thinking it was a large barn owl or something."

I could feel the goose bumps traveling up my arms again. "This thing that I saw stood as tall as you. I couldn't make out what it looked like, but it was something much larger than a bird."

"Hopefully, these cameras will pick something up. They have a range of one hundred feet. I'll make sure some of them are pointing towards the woods, too."

When we made it back to the cabin, it was almost five o'clock and my mother was gone.

"Wow, nice place," said Duncan.

"It is. Too bad I'm not enjoying it because I'm so freaked out at night."

"I don't blame you."

I showed him around the cabin and then he started unloading the truck.

"Um, is there a way that you can put a camera near my bedroom balcony?" I asked.

"Have you seen someone looking through it?" he asked, incredulously.

"Actually, I thought I saw someone staring at me through the window in my bathroom when I was getting out of the tub."

He raised his eyebrows. "He actually saw you naked?"

My face turned pink. "I think so."

Duncan smiled wickedly. "I guess it would be inappropriate for me to say, 'Lucky man'?"

My jaw dropped and I smiled. "Uh, yeah!"

"I'm sorry, I just couldn't resist."

"Right."

"I'm sorry, that was uncalled for; a feeble attempt to flirt."

"You were trying to flirt with me?"

His gray eyes burned into mine. "I was. Did it work?"

I shivered in pleasure. "Well, I..."

Thankfully, Nathan pulled up in his car at that moment and I was saved from having to answer anything.

"Hey, guys," he said, slamming the door.

"Hi," said Duncan, walking past him. "Nikki just gave me a tour of the place, so let's start getting these things set up before it gets dark."

"Sounds good," replied Nathan.

"Where's the dry cleaning?" I whispered.

He smiled sheepishly. "Oh, I must have forgotten it."

"You did that on purpose. Thanks," I said, sarcastically.

"You're welcome. Did you guys make out, yet?"

I punched him in the shoulder.

Chapter Eleven

It took a couple of hours to set up all of the cameras. Mom showed up just as we were finishing up.

"What's all this?" she asked.

Nathan explained that we were setting up surveillance to catch a Peeping Tom.

"I thought we were through with that?" she said. She was wearing dark sunglasses and looked like she was still suffering from her hangover.

I cleared my throat. "Duncan had someone looking in his windows last night, too, mom. It's not just us."

She raised her eyebrows. "Really?"

Duncan nodded. "Yeah and it was definitely not an animal."

Mom yawned. "Then I hope you catch whoever is doing it. It's probably some pervert or something."

"Or a killer," I said.

"What?" she asked, incredulously. She'd obviously heard me but didn't believe what I was suggesting.

"Nothing."

She yawned again. "Listen, I'm going to lie down for a while. I'm so wiped out."

"Do you want me to make dinner?" I asked.

She grimaced. "Actually, I've been nauseated all day. I'm going to eat a couple more crackers and then go right to bed."

"Duncan, would you like to dine with us?" asked Nathan as mom trudged up the stairs and into the cabin. "I make a mean frozen pizza."

Duncan laughed. "No, I have to head back before my old man starts hounding me again," he said, raising his cell phone. "He's already sent me a message, wondering where I am."

"Okay, thanks for setting all of this up. I kind of hope we see some action tonight," said Nathan.

"Here's my number," he said, holding out a business card. "My dad made these for me to give to customers. Call me if something happens."

"Will do. Your dad has my number, call me if you catch a prowler."

"Okay. Good luck with your new job, Nikki," said Duncan. "I'll give you a couple of days before I stop in and harass you."

"Thanks."

After Duncan left, we walked around the perimeter of the house again to make sure all of the cameras were facing the right way.

"There's even one by your balcony to make sure some Romeo doesn't try and steal you away at night."

I snorted. "If someone shows up on my balcony, I'm going to beat them with my bat while I scream bloody murder."

He laughed. "That guy has no chance."

We went into the kitchen where Nathan made a pizza and then joined me on the couch to watch movies.

"So what do you think of mom dating Caleb?" I asked.

"He seems like a good guy."

"You don't think it's too soon for her?"

"I think mom is lonely and wants to feel protected. The town's sheriff sure fits that bill."

I shrugged. "I suppose. I'm just worried about her getting hurt."

"Nobody can hurt her as much as dad did," said Nathan. "Sad but true."

That was for certain.

I fell asleep halfway through some horror flick about zombies when several loud thuds from outside woke me up.

"What was that?" I gasped.

Nathan stood up and I could tell he was as freaked out as I was. "I don't know."

Something heavy banged against the door, and we both jumped.

"Oh, my God, Nathan, what's happening?"

He ran into the kitchen and came back out carrying the butcher knife.

"You're not going out there, are you?" I whispered in horror.

He swallowed. "I was considering it."

More loud bangs and I grabbed the phone. "I'm calling nine-one-one."

"Wait, it could be a raccoon or a bear."

"A bear; like you'd want to tackle that by yourself, anyway."

He nodded. "True. I'm going to open up the blinds and look outside."

I followed him over to the window. "Can you see anything?" I asked as he peeked through the gap in the blinds.

"Shit," he whispered.

"What?"

He turned towards me, his face as white as a ghost. "It's the cameras. Un... fucking... believable!"

I looked outside and gasped. Even in the dark I could tell that someone had destroyed all of the surveillance equipment we'd set up.

We raced upstairs and woke up mom. She called the police, and a half hour later, one of the deputy sheriffs arrived at the house.

"I don't know who did this, but they're gone now," he said. He was a middle-aged man with a curly black moustache that he kept touching, which creeped me out.

Mom let out a long, ragged sigh. "Why would somebody do this?"

"Oh, I don't know... so they wouldn't get caught spying on *us*?" I muttered sarcastically.

"Can you check for fingerprints or anything?" asked Nathan.

He nodded. "Yeah, I put a call in for a couple of our guys to get out here and do that, so try not to touch anything. They should be arriving any minute."

"So, where is the sheriff?" I asked.

"Caleb? Oh, it's his night off," replied the deputy. "He won't be back in until late tomorrow night."

Mom nodded. "He mentioned that he was going out of town today with his daughter."

"Let me get a statement from you and then I'll be on my way. There isn't much we can do without any evidence right now. If we pick up something from the fingerprints, we'll proceed from there."

After everyone was gone, mom dragged herself back to bed but Nathan and I were still spooked and unable to sleep.

Nathan shook his head. "Duncan is going to be pissed when he finds out what happened. That was thousands of dollars in video equipment this person destroyed."

"Let's call him, it's only eleven. I'm sure he's awake."

A half hour later Duncan pulled up in his white truck. Our eyes met immediately and I had to admit, I was really glad to see him.

"Wow," he said, "This is amazing. I can't believe someone trashed all of these cameras. Did you see anything?"

"We heard the crashes but were too freaked out to investigate when it was happening," I said. "It actually happened pretty quickly."

"They must have brought their own ladder," said Nathan. "I locked up the other one we'd used, earlier."

Duncan walked over to one of the trees and smiled proudly. "They missed one. I hid it pretty good. Let's go see if it recorded anything interesting."

Nathan slapped him on the back. "You are the man!"

Fifteen minutes later, we stared in awe at the video screen.

"What in the hell?" asked Nathan.

We watched in disbelief, as two of the other cameras were violently ripped from the house, but there was no sign of whoever was doing it.

"Ghosts?" I gasped incredulously. "I mean, there's nobody there!"

Duncan and Nathan looked at each other, both obviously stunned as well.

"This is freaking crazy. It doesn't make sense," said Nathan.

We rewound the video and watched it again with the same results. It seemed as if an invisible force had destroyed each of the cameras.

"Okay, common sense doesn't explain this at all," said Duncan. "Maybe it is some kind of poltergeist?"

"If it is, I'm definitely not staying here any longer," I said. The thought of the cabin being inhabited by ghosts freaked the crap out of me. I saw the movies Poltergeist and Amityville Horror. I knew when it was time to leave. Not after the ghosts tried killing you, but before.

"We have to show the sheriff," said Nathan. "Maybe he can make sense of it."

"Sense? A fucking ghost is messing with our minds, Nathan," I snapped. "You keep trying to make scientific excuses because you don't want to believe it. Look at the film! You heard the loud bangs! The cameras didn't just fall from the house by themselves! We've got to get the hell out of this town!"

He raised his hands. "Okay, calm down. You're right. Something is happening that is beyond any explanation that I can come up with. We'll show mom tomorrow and still talk to the sheriff. If it is some kind of ghost, we'll get the cabin... exorcised or something "

"Maybe you should talk to the owners of the cabin?" interrupted Duncan. "They might already be aware of these ghosts."

"What about your house, Duncan?" I asked. "How do you explain the face in the window or shadows flying into the trees?"

He smiled wryly. "Maybe the ghost is roaming the town? I don't know. None of this shit makes sense to me, either."

We watched the video one last time and then Duncan turned it off. "I'm going home to check on the cameras I've installed there, to see if they're still in place. I'll call you if I find anything else odd."

"Duncan," I said. "I'm sorry about the damaged equipment. I wish we could somehow replace it for you."

He waved his hand. "Hell, it's not your fault. If anything, we may have actual proof that ghosts inhabit Shore Lake," he said with a sinister smile. "We could all become rich and famous."

Chapter Twelve

I woke up around nine-thirty the next morning and noticed that mom was still sleeping.

"She must be coming down with something," I said to Nathan, who was outside sweeping up pieces of the broken video equipment.

He shrugged. "Could be the fresh air."

"Maybe. So, did you hear anything from Duncan yet?"

"Yeah, he said his cameras were fine and there didn't appear to be anything unusual going on in the videos."

"That's good, I guess. I had a hard time sleeping last night. I felt like something was watching me again."

He laughed. "Probably me. I checked up on you a couple of times and you were snoring away."

"I do not snore."

"How in the hell do you know?"

I raised my chin. "I just do."

He snorted. "Whatever. Anyway, as soon as mom gets up, we'll show her the video and see what she thinks."

Just then, an old red pickup drove up the path and parked next to Nathan's Mustang.

"It's our neighbor. I think mom said her name's Abigail," said Nathan.

"Hello!" said the older woman, getting out of the truck. "I just wanted to stop by and welcome you. Sorry it took me so long."

"No problem," said Nathan. "We should have come over and introduced ourselves."

"No worries," she replied, carrying a large pie pan. "I hope you like strawberry rhubarb pie; I made it fresh, early this morning!"

"We love it, thank you," said Nathan as she handed it to him. "Wow, it looks awesome."

"My name is Abigail, by the way. I live at the next cabin over."

"I'm Nathan and that's Nikki," said Nathan.

"Hi," I said.

"Wonderful to meet you both."

Abigail looked like she was in her seventies or eighties, had reddish-brown hair and watery green eyes.

"I'll be right back," said Nathan. "I'll put the pie in the kitchen. Did you want a piece, Abigail?"

She shook her head and smiled. "No, but thank you. I made it for you folks."

"Okay, if you change your mind, let me know," he called, going into the house.

"Um, our mother's not feeling well," I explained. "Otherwise she'd be out here greeting you, too. I'm sure she'll be sad that she missed you."

She smiled. "That's all right."

"I suppose you saw the police here a couple of times," I said.

Her smile fell. "Yes I did notice that."

"We found a body the first night we arrived, and last night, someone smashed our video equipment. We've been trying to catch the culprit. It's been pretty crazy."

"A body?" she said, her eyes widening. "Was it that young girl they mentioned on the news? Tina Johnson?"

I nodded. "Yes. They think she drowned and washed up here."

"They don't think it's... foul play?"

"Well," I said. "Personally, I think it is, but nobody else seems to believe it."

She leaned forward. "And why do you think it's foul play?"

I sighed. "Because we've had someone trying to scare us every night since we arrived. Then, the waitress who supposedly killed herself in the woods the other night, Amy? She gave me a warning the same day she died."

"What do you mean?"

"She slipped me a note at Ruth's, warning me not to go out at night and not to let any strangers into our home."

Abigail stared at me for a few seconds and then let out a long sigh. "Nikki, she gave you some good advice. If I were you, I'd stay in and not invite anyone into your cabin. Especially, those you don't know."

My heart began to pound. "So, you think it's dangerous out here at night?"

Her eyes grew misty. "I know it is. My husband was killed by something evil," she said, looking up at towards trees. "There are things in Shore Lake that you don't know about; things you couldn't even imagine. In fact, I wanted to come over and warn you myself, before I left town."

"What do you mean?" I asked, the hair standing up on the back of my neck.

Just then, Nathan walked out. "Okay, I couldn't resist, Abigail; I had a little piece. And let me tell you, it was the best strawberry rhubarb pie I'd ever tasted."

She nodded. "Good."

Noticing her sudden melancholy, he asked, "Are you okay?"

"Um, Nathan, Abigail was just telling me it's dangerous here at night and that her husband was murdered."

Nathan's stared at her in horror. "Your husband was murdered? Do you know who did it?"

"Vampires," she stated without hesitation.

"Excuse me?" choked Nathan.

Her face darkened. "Shore Lake is infested with vampires."

He burst out laughing and clapped his hands. "Okay, very funny, Abigail. Vampires, that's a good one!"

The look in her eyes was so serious, it made me start to doubt what was real and what wasn't.

"Don't mock me," she said. "I'm not joking, young man."

The porch door opened up and mom stepped out. She was wearing dark sunglasses and still looked unusually pale.

"Hey, mom," said Nathan. "This is Abigail."

Mom nodded. "Yes, I remember seeing you fishing the other day. Nice to meet you, Abigail. I'm Anne."

"Nice to meet you, too. Say, if you don't mind my asking, what's wrong with your neck?"

The swelling on mom's neck appeared to be getting worse. She touched it and winced. "I don't know. I think I was bitten by a couple of mosquitos, or maybe even a spider."

Abigail cleared her throat. "I used to be a nurse, can I take a look?"

"Sure," replied mom.

Abigail walked up onto the porch and examined the bites. After a few seconds she stepped back. "When did you get those?"

Mom shrugged. "I don't know, the other night when the sheriff was over for dinner. I didn't notice it until the next morning."

"Sheriff Caleb?" asked Abigail.

"Yes, the sheriff," I said. "I guess you could say they're dating."

Abigail backed away from mom and then hurried down the porch. "I have to go. It was nice meeting you folks."

"What's wrong?" I asked. First her talk about vampires, and now she appeared to be spooked by the bites on mom's neck. Then it hit me. "You're not thinking that the bites on mom's neck are... vampire bites, are you?" I asked with a wry smile. Even I had a hard time believing her ridiculous talk. Believing in ghosts was bad enough.

She opened her truck door and turned back to look at us. "Damn right I do."

Chapter Thirteen

"What?" chuckled mom, staring at her in disbelief.

She pointed towards her neck. "You've got the mark and if you don't get out of town while you still can, you'll be a threat to your children and everyone else in town."

All of us watched her in stunned silence as she slammed the door and drove away, kicking up dust in her wake.

"Now *that* was really weird," I said.

"What a fruitcake," said mom as she turned around and headed back into the house. "Certifiable nutcase."

I followed her in and we went into the kitchen.

"So, um… are you feeling, okay?" I asked.

She removed her sunglasses and smiled. "I feel like turning into a vampire and sucking your blood!" she joked.

I snorted. "Yeah, that was one weird old lady. Maybe she's the one trying to scare us."

She sighed. "You know, I never thought of that. I should mention it to Caleb when he comes over tonight."

"Are you guys going on a real date this time, or are you cooking, again?"

"Actually, he's planning on bringing me to his place. His daughter is making dinner for both of us, I guess."

"Mom," said Nathan, coming into the kitchen. "Did Nikki tell you yet?"

"Tell me what?"

Nathan told her about the video and she followed us into the den to watch it.

"Something must be wrong with the camera," said mom. "There's no way that video equipment fell to the ground on its own."

"Or… we have a poltergeist," I said.

She looked at me and groaned. "You've got to be kidding! First all this talk about vampires, and now, you, with the ghosts?"

"Then how do you explain what happened on the film?" said Nathan. "Even I'm having a little trouble with it."

She closed her eyes and rubbed the bridge of her nose. "Seriously, I don't know. Maybe Duncan didn't fasten them down tight enough and they fell. Or maybe an animal pulled them down."

"I think we should show them to the sheriff and see what he thinks," said Nathan.

"Okay, he'll be here after nine o'clock to pick me up. I'll show him."

"You hungry, mom?" asked Nathan. "I can make you something."

"Could you? I'm starving," she said. "I'll go take a shower and you can make me whatever you want."

"Okay, how about a hamburger?" he asked.

She yawned. "Oh, now that sounds good."

"How do you want it prepared?"

Mom turned to him and smiled wickedly. "Bloody rare. I'm turning into a vampire, you know."

~~~

I spent most of the day watching television and thinking about Duncan. He was coming over tonight when I was finished at the diner, and all three of us were going to try and videotape some more ghost activity. Nathan now believed it was really a poltergeist and was even talking about hiring an expert to help us.

Nathan dropped me off at the diner just before four o'clock. It was busy and the waitress who was supposed to train me, Susan, appeared stressed out.

"Just follow me around for now and when it slows up, I'll go over the menus and tickets," she said, stepping around me with a tray full of food.

"Okay."

I followed her to a busy table while other customers tried getting her attention. She handed out the food and then I followed her back to the counter, where she handed me a coffeepot.

"Better idea, why don't you just go around and see if any of my tables need coffee or soda refills?" she said, pointing to her section.

Unfortunately, it never did slow down and I spent most of my time following her around or refilling beverages. At the end of the night, my feet were sore, but Susan had shared some of her tips, so I was happy.

"Sorry the training sucked today," she said, removing her apron. "We've been so busy ever since Amy…" she looked away.

I nodded. "I understand."

She turned back to me and her eyes were moist. "She was a good friend. It's going to be hard to replace her."

"I doubt I could ever replace her," I said. "In fact, she was the one who gave me the application in the first place."

"Listen, if you can stay a little later tomorrow night, I'll go over everything else with you that we missed during our shift. Friday evenings are always busy, so plan on being here, late."

"Okay, thanks."

"Just remember two of the most important rules: the customer is always right, even when they're wrong, and to always smile, even when you want to slit their throats. Especially the super picky customers."

I smiled. "Okay."

She stared at me for a minute.

"What?" I asked.

"You know, you look very similar to Amy. Different color hair, but your features are similar."

My cell phone began to vibrate.

"It's my ride," I told her and answered the phone.

"Hi," said Nathan. "My car won't start."

"What do you mean?"

He sighed. "The battery must be dead or something. I'm trying to get ahold of Duncan, to see if he can give you a ride home."

"What about mom?"

"I can't find her keys anywhere. Caleb's already picked her up, and she forgot her cell phone here on the counter."

"Great. Okay, let me know if you talk to Duncan. I'll just hang out here for a while."

I hung up the phone and Susan tapped me on the shoulder. "Sorry, I wasn't trying to listen in but… do you need a ride?"

"I might."

"My brother should be here in a half hour. I'm sure he'll give you one."

I smiled. "Thanks. I can't wait until I get my own car. Relying on someone else for a ride all the time is so frustrating."

"I know. I'm going outside to have a smoke, you want to join me?"

"I don't smoke but I'll come out with you"

We both grabbed a couple of sodas and I followed her out the back door of the diner where there was a picnic table. We sat down in the darkness and she cleared her throat. "At least it's a nice night. The moon is full and there aren't any clouds."

It was true; the stars were bright and it was a little cool outside, so we weren't getting bitten up by mosquitos. It seemed really peaceful, although I kept thinking about Amy and her warnings about how dangerous it was at night in Shore Lake.

Susan lit up a cigarette and took a long drag. "Oh, man, I needed that."

"So… you were friends with Amy?" I asked.

"Yeah," she said, looking away. "I still can't believe she's gone."

"She seemed really nice when I met her."

Susan looked at me and nodded. "She *was* a sweetheart. Her boyfriend, though, he was scary. I'm glad she dumped him."

"She had a boyfriend?"

She blew out another stream of smoke. "Yeah, Ethan. He hangs out here sometimes at night with his crew. They're all kind of freaky if you ask me."

"Why, what do you mean?"

Susan shrugged. "I don't know; there's just something strange about them. They come in here, hardly saying a word to each other. They just sit and stare at us, sipping their coffee. Ethan is the scariest. He's cute, but there's something about him that makes me nervous. He has these penetrating blue eyes that give me the creeps. Anyway, I really hate serving them, but they're paying customers, so we can't exactly kick them out."

I cleared my throat. "Weird. So, why did she break up with this Ethan guy?"

She laughed. "Amy always had quite the imagination. Everyone thought she was a little… nuts, and maybe, she really was. I mean, she did kill herself. Anyway, she once told me she thought he was a vampire."

"What?" I choked on my diet soda.

"I know, right?" she smirked. "A freakin' vampire! Although, if I did believe in vampires, he'd be the first on my list of suspects."

My throat was really dry as I took another sip of soda. First Abigail, and now Amy; both believed there were vampires roaming the town.

"We'd better go back into the diner," she said, putting out her cigarette. "My brother will be here soon. I'll see if he can give you a ride."

My cell phone went off again as we entered the diner.

"It's Nathan," said my brother. "Duncan's coming to pick you up."

"Great, thanks," I said.

"Make sure he brings you straight home. Don't go jumping his bones or anything."

"Ha-ha. You are such a comedian."

He laughed and hung up.

"I'm getting a ride from a friend," I told Susan. "Thanks for the offer, though."

"No problem. Oh, my brother's here," she said, looking at her phone. "He just texted me. I'll see you tomorrow, at four o'clock again?"

"Yeah, see you tomorrow."

After she left, I sat down at one of the booths, to finish my soda and wait for Duncan. As I watched the front door, a group of kids around my age walked through. One of the other waitresses seated them.

"Same as usual?" asked the older waitress, who I'd met earlier. Her name was Darlene and she was close to retiring.

"Just coffee," said a broad-shouldered, dark-haired guy, ordering for everyone. He handed her back the menu and our eyes met.

Embarrassed, I looked away quickly and stared outside at the parking lot, watching for Duncan.

Before I could blink, someone slid into my booth and I was suddenly facing the stranger whose eyes I'd just met.

"Um, hi," I said, sitting up straighter.

"Um, hi, yourself," he said with a slow, lazy grin.

Oh wow...

"I'm Nikki," I replied, feeling myself blush at the intense way he was staring at me. I knew it had to be Amy's ex-boyfriend, and he was undoubtedly gorgeous. He had thick, dark eyebrows with icy blue eyes; his face was perfectly sculpted with high cheekbones and a strong chin. His lips... they were sensual and even fuller than mine.

"You're new in town?"

"Yes," I replied, now studying his face more closely. He was definitely a little pale, which reminded me of the fact that Amy had accused him of being vampire. As I stared at him, I reasoned that most girls my age would have swooned at such a good-looking guy, but after everything that had happened the last few nights, I felt a cold shiver run down my spine.

"Welcome to Shore Lake," he replied, looking into my eyes again.

"Thanks."

It was weird, but we sat there and stared at each other for a while without talking. Soon, I started feeling a heat somewhere inside of my belly that turned into an overwhelming ache of desire, further south.

"I, ah..." My heart was pounding in my chest and I felt a strong urge to touch him. It was almost overwhelming.

"Nikki," interrupted Duncan, standing next to our table. "Are you ready to go?"

I looked at Duncan and the spell, or whatever it was, was broken. "Yeah," I said. "I'm ready."

"Goodbye, Nikki," said Ethan, with a small grin. "I'm sure we'll meet again."

"Goodbye," I murmured, looking away. I was confused at the intense rush of desire I'd had for Ethan. He was a total stranger. How did that even happen?

"Who was that?" asked Duncan as he followed me out to his truck.

I don't know how I knew, but there was no doubt in my mind that Ethan was still staring at me through the window. I shivered and wrapped my arms around myself. "You might think I'm crazy, but I'm pretty sure he was a vampire."

Chapter Fourteen

"Excuse me?" he asked, unlocking the truck.

We both slid inside and I looked at him. "Amy was convinced he was a vampire, and there's something about him that's totally... unnerving."

He shook his head and smiled as he started up the truck. "Okay, your imagination is really getting the best of you. It's bad enough that there might be a ghost haunting your cabin, but a vampire in the local diner?"

I nodded. "I feel the same way, but there was something so strange about him. He made me feel..."

He raised his eyebrows. "He made you feel what?"

I swallowed hard. "Um, weird."

I wasn't about to tell Duncan that at one moment, I wanted to jump Ethan's bones and probably would have, if we'd been alone. It didn't even make sense to me.

Duncan looked back towards the diner. "If he gives you any problems, let me know."

I smiled. "Sure."

We pulled out of the parking lot in silence as I thought about the strange encounter. Duncan glanced at me a couple of times, and I could tell there was something on his mind, as well.

"What's wrong?" I asked him.

He pulled over to the side of the road.

"What is it, Duncan?"

He tapped the steering wheel a couple of times and then looked at me. There was a funny smile on his face. "When I approached you with Ethan, you almost looked like you were ready to tear his clothes off or something. I don't know; it just made me feel a little… jealous."

I'm not even sure how it happened, but the next thing I knew, I was straddling him in the front seat and our mouths were crushed against each other.

"Nikki," he groaned against my lips.

My heart was pounding madly in my chest and I rocked against him, causing him to suck in his breath. He pulled away and looked into my eyes.

"I don't think…" he whispered.

"Don't think," I said breathlessly, pulling him back towards my lips. There was an intense hunger inside of me, one that I'd never felt before. I wanted to tear off both of our clothing, just so I could feel our skin moving against each other.

His mouth was hot, and soon he was kissing my neck while his hands moved under my shirt. As he was about to slide his fingers under my bra, my cell phone rang, startling us both. He quickly removed his hands and I got off of his lap.

My face was burning with embarrassment as I fumbled for my phone. "Yeah?" I said into it, unable to look at Duncan.

"Hello to you, too," mumbled Nathan.

I cleared my throat. "Sorry."

"You guys almost home, yet?"

I nervously bit off a hangnail. "Almost."

"Okay, I ordered a pizza and it's already here, so hurry the hell up."

I hung up and stole a glance at Duncan.

"I'm sorry," he said, although his eyes were still smoldering. "I don't know what came over me."

I smiled sheepishly. "I, um… it was me. I practically raped you. I've never done that before, to anyone. I'm sorry."

"At least I know you like me."

I burst out laughing. "Do you think?"

"I'm sure you could probably tell that I liked you, too," he said, grinning.

My cheeks grew hot and I changed the subject. "So, I hope you're hungry. Nathan has a pizza waiting for us."

"Oh, I'm starving, alright," he said under his breath.

I looked at him and sighed. "Duncan, I…"

He stared at me for a minute. "It's okay," he said. "I'm not in a rush for anything."

I smiled. "Thank you. I really do like you, you know. I'm just…"

He held up his hand. "Hey, it's okay."

It wasn't okay. I really liked Duncan but I'd never attacked anyone before in my life like that. It was almost like the burning desire I'd felt towards Ethan had carried over towards Duncan. I was beginning to wonder if Ethan really was a vampire and had given off some kind of weird pheromone.

We rode in silence the rest of the way to the cabin. Nathan was sitting on the porch, holding a BB gun, when we arrived.

"We come in peace," teased Duncan, raising his hands in the air.

Nathan grinned. "Sorry. I was beginning to freak myself out, so I grabbed my old BB gun. I thought I heard some noises in the woods. But then, I actually found a couple of raccoons prowling around."

"Is the video camera still set up?" asked Duncan.

"Yeah. I think we should hang out on Nikki's balcony and watch from above. See if we can see anyone sneaking around," said Nathan. "Just in case it isn't a ghost, but some jackass trying to screw with us."

"Good idea," replied Duncan.

We went inside, grabbed the box of pizza and some plates, and then headed up to my bedroom. On the balcony, Nathan had set up three chairs and a bistro table. We sat down and started eating.

"How was work?" asked Nathan.

"Busy. I met this girl named Susan who was friends with Amy."

"Is she cute?" asked Nathan.

"God, is that all you think about?" I asked.

"Is there anything else, Dunc?"

Duncan smiled but didn't say anything.

"Anyway, Susan was telling me that Amy believed her ex-boyfriend, Ethan, was a vampire."

Nathan snorted. "Yeah, I'd say Amy was a little messed up."

"I don't know," I said, staring at my pizza.

His eyes narrowed. "What do you mean, *you don't know?*"

I swallowed. "I met Ethan tonight and there was something really strange about him."

"He was dating Amy at one point, that tells you enough right there," said Nathan.

"No, he came over and sat by me at the restaurant. When he looked into my eyes, I almost felt like... I was under some kind of spell."

"How do you mean?" asked Nathan.

"I can't explain it," I said, looking sideways at Duncan. There was no way I was going to explain my desire to jump

Ethan's bones, especially after what had happened between us, in the truck.

Nathan sat back and groaned. "There is no such thing as vampires, period. Quit letting Abigail's and Amy's crazy notions play with your mind. I mean, come on, Nikki, you know better than that!"

I shrank down in my seat. "I know. It's just…I can't explain it."

Nathan looked at Duncan. "What do you think about all of this?"

Duncan shrugged. "I don't know. I think something strange is going on and I'm not ruling anything out."

Nathan snorted. "Even vampires?"

"Maybe this Ethan guy believes he's a vampire and knows how to manipulate other people into believing it, too."

"That sounds more reasonable to me. Maybe he knows how to actually hypnotize people. That would explain how Nikki believed she was under some kind of spell."

"Maybe," I answered.

We sat in silence, as we finished the pizza and stared towards the woods. It was pretty silent except for the leaves rustling in the wind.

"Anyone want something to drink?" asked Nathan, standing up.

"I'll take some water," I said.

"Me, too," answered Duncan.

When Nathan left us alone, I stole a glance towards Duncan, who I found was staring at me.

"What?" I asked.

He smiled. "I was just thinking how beautiful you looked in the moonlight. I know that sounds like a line, but it's true."

I returned his smile. "Thanks, Duncan."

He clasped his fingers and rested his chin on them. "Did you leave a broken heart back in California?"

105

I snorted. "No. In fact, I guess you could say I haven't had many boyfriends."

"I find that hard to believe. The guys there must be blind and stupid."

I blushed. "It's not like I didn't get asked out. I just wasn't interested, I guess."

"So, would you be interested now?"

I nodded.

He smiled.

"Duncan," said Nathan, as he stepped onto the balcony. "I almost forgot, could you take a look at my Mustang? I think it's the battery I'm having problems with, but I want to make sure."

"Do you have a battery tester?" he asked.

"Actually, there might be one in the garage, I never even looked."

Duncan got up. "Let's go and check it out."

Nathan nodded. "Thanks. Nikki, you can keep watch from up here and let us know if you see anything. I brought you the BB gun," he said, handing it to me. "You still know how to use it?"

"Yeah."

"Okay. Holler if you see anything," he said.

They left me and I gripped the gun firmly in my hands, feeling uneasy because I was now alone and they were going to be in the garage.

Nathan's laughter echoed through the darkness. I watched as the guys stepped away from the cabin and headed over to the garage.

"Nothing to be afraid of," I murmured to myself, staring towards the dark woods.

An owl hooted and I was reminded of some of the scary movies I'd watched with Nathan. An owl hoots and then something sinister usually happens in the next scene. I knew it was just cinema, but I felt a chill in my veins just the same.

My eyes darted quickly from one side of the yard to the other, and my breath caught in my throat as I saw a shadow move across the grass. I looked up into the sky, but saw nothing out of the ordinary.

"Nikki," whispered a deep masculine voice behind me.

I turned around, but found myself alone. I stood up and backed away from the table, frightened beyond belief. Hot breath brushed against the back of my neck and I whirled around again, this time seeing a blurry haze of movement.

"Oh, my God... Nathan!" I screamed, running into my bedroom. I ran downstairs and threw the front door open. "Nathan!" I yelled, again.

Nathan and Duncan rushed out of the garage towards me.

"What's wrong?" called Nathan.

"Someone... was... on the balcony," I gasped, out of breath.

He looked behind me. "Who?"

I shook my head. "I don't know. I heard my name and then I felt someone breathing against the back of my neck."

"Someone's in the cabin?" Nathan swore, and then rushed past me and towards the house.

Duncan could tell I was pretty shook up and put his arms around me. He stared down into my eyes. "Are you okay?"

I nodded and leaned into him, closing my eyes.

Suddenly, he was ripped from my arms and thrown backwards.

"Duncan!" I screamed as he landed on the ground.

"I'm fine," he answered with an incredulous look on his face. He got up and began walking back towards me.

There was a flash of movement and he went flying through the air again, much farther this time. As I rushed towards him, I felt something pick me up, and then we were moving like the wind.

"Help!" I screamed in terror. We were going so fast that my head was spinning. The next thing I knew I was lying on the ground and a pair of steely blue eyes held mine.

"We meet again," whispered Ethan, trailing a cool finger down my cheek.

I was paralyzed as his eyes burned into mine. A familiar yearning spread through my veins and suddenly I wanted him fiercely.

"Sweet Nikki," he whispered with a small smile. He then licked his lips and lowered them to mine. Suddenly, we were kissing and I felt an urgent need to wrap my legs around him; to surrender myself to whatever he demanded.

"Oh," I breathed when he removed his mouth and began a hot trail down my neck with his tongue. My entire body was trembling with desire. "Oh, God."

He chuckled softly against my skin. "Not quite."

Someone shouted my name, startling me back to my senses and I tensed up.

Duncan!

Ethan raised his head and I could see the rage burning in his eyes. "Fuck," he growled.

Duncan crashed through the bushes right as Ethan took off and I was left staring up at the stars in confusion.

"Are you okay?" asked Duncan, now at my side, looking down at me.

"I think so," I replied, as he helped me up.

"What in the hell just happened!" hollered Nathan, stumbling through the woods, out of breath.

My lips began to tremble. "I really don't know."

Chapter Fifteen

Nathan and Duncan were full of questions as we walked back to the house. I was still in a state of confusion and had a difficult time answering them.

"Who was it?" asked Duncan.

"Where'd they go?" asked Nathan.

I shook my head. "I...I just can't remember."

It wasn't exactly true, but my thoughts were so muddled because of my overwhelming attraction towards Ethan. Part of me understood that it wasn't natural; it was some power he was using to control me. Another part of me didn't care; I just wanted him to have his way with me, whatever it was.

Nathan scratched his head. "Did you see who it was, Duncan?"

He shook his head. "I was thrown backwards and then she was gone in a flash. It was crazy."

Nathan scowled. "I don't even know how to call this one in to nine-one-one. Attempted kidnapping by the invisible man?"

I cleared my throat. "Um, don't worry about it, Nathan. I'm fine."

"No, we have to call the police. You could have been murdered or raped."

It certainly wouldn't have been rape, I thought. Although, if he was using mind control to make me desire him so much, then it was as bad as a date rape drug.

"I didn't see anything. I don't even know who it was," I protested. "The cops are going to think we're all crazy."

Nathan stared at me for a minute. "Okay, I'd better ask – was it human?"

"To be honest, I don't know," I muttered.

Duncan grabbed my hand. "I'm calling my dad to let him know I'm staying over tonight. I'm not letting you out of my sight again."

Nathan looked at both of us. "Wait a second, did I miss something?"

I could feel my cheeks turn pink.

"I guess you could say that I'm kind of falling for your sister," said Duncan with a sheepish grin. "I hope you're okay with it."

Nathan smiled. "I'm fine with it. Now I won't be the only guy who has to suffer her P.M.S."

I slugged him in the shoulder. "Very funny, booger."

"See," he said, moving away from my fist, which was cocked again.

"Heads-up, your mom's home," said Duncan.

She was just getting out of the sheriff's car and he was helping her up the stairs.

"Sheriff, what's wrong with her?" asked Nathan.

Caleb smiled. "She enjoyed one too many glasses of wine again. I brought her home so she could sleep."

Mom gave us a lopsided grin. "Hi, my babies…"

I groaned.

She was totally hammered and stumbled towards me. "Nikki, I love you."

Nathan and I put our arms around her and held her up. "Wow, mom," I grunted, trying to hold her up. "I think it's time you start laying off the vino."

Her smile fell. "I didn't have anything to drink."

"Sure you did," interrupted the sheriff. "Don't you remember the Cabernet you picked out yourself from the wine cellar? We had it with dinner."

Mom looked confused but then when her eyes met Caleb's, she smiled wickedly and licked her lips. "All, I remember is dessert."

"Okay, T.M.I.," I replied as Nathan and I swung her away from Caleb and into the house. The idea of her and Caleb getting it on was enough to make me want to be celibate for life.

"I'll call you tomorrow night!" called Caleb from the porch.

"Nikki, can you take care of mom? I'm going to talk to the sheriff," said Nathan.

I nodded and then proceeded to help her upstairs, which wasn't an easy task. When we finally made it to her bedroom, she passed out the moment her head hit the pillow. I removed her shoes and covered her up with a sheet as she began to snore.

"Nikki, the sheriff wants to talk to you," said Duncan, as I closed mom's bedroom door.

I nodded and took his hand while he led me back downstairs. Both Nathan and Caleb were sitting on the couch.

"So, I heard there was a little excitement here earlier?" asked Caleb.

I sighed. "I guess you could say that. It was really… bizarre."

He nodded and took out a notepad. "Could you tell me in your words what happened?"

I gave him my version but left off the part of knowing who the person was that carried me off.

Caleb's eyes narrowed. "So, you didn't get a good look at the person at all? Didn't notice what he was wearing or what he even smelled like?"

Come to think of it, Ethan had smelled like butterscotch.

I rubbed my arm. "To tell you the truth, I was so scared that I didn't notice much of anything. I do know that he was as fast as the wind."

Duncan nodded. "He was quick. He shoved me to the ground, twice, and I didn't see him either; just a blur of movement."

Sheriff Caleb put away the notes he was taking and smiled wryly. "You realize how this sounds, don't you?"

Nathan nodded. "Crazy, I know."

"I know, show him the video," said Duncan.

"Oh, yeah," replied Nathan, grabbing the tape from the fireplace mantel. "We taped this yesterday after someone destroyed all the video surveillance equipment. They apparently missed this one."

We all watched the video in silence, and when it was over, Caleb let out a long sigh.

Nathan folded his arms across his chest. "Even crazier, huh?"

He nodded. "I don't really know what to say about it, actually. It doesn't really make a lot of sense."

I cleared my throat. "What should we do?"

Caleb ran a hand over his face. "Let me take this tape and I'll show some friends who specialize in paranormal research."

Nathan's jaw dropped. "So you think it might be a poltergeist, too?"

He shrugged. "Even I have to admit; it's *some* kind of strange phenomenon. I just have no experience with this type of thing."

"Okay, yeah take it. Let us know what you find out," said Nathan, giving him the tape.

Caleb stood up and started walking towards the door. "What about Nikki?" asked Duncan. "How are we supposed to protect her against whatever this thing is?"

Caleb turned back and looked at us. "Don't go anywhere alone, keep your doors locked, and don't invite any strangers in."

Chapter Sixteen

Nathan and Duncan slept on my bedroom floor that night, just in case the "specter" came back to harass me. When I woke up, it was just after nine the next morning and I was alone. I went down to the kitchen.

"Where's Duncan?" I asked.

As usual, Nathan was stuffing his face with food. "He had to work. He's going to pick you up after your shift again tonight. I'll get mom's keys and drop you off at four."

"Did you guys ever figure out what's wrong with the Mustang?"

He nodded. "It's the battery. I'm picking up a new one today."

I yawned. "Where's mom? Still sleeping?"

He nodded. "Yeah, she's been doing a lot of that lately. I think she should quit drinking, she just can't handle it."

"I agree."

Plus, she was our mom and really not making a good impression by getting so hammered.

Two hours later, mom was still sleeping so I decided to check up on her.

"Mom?" I called, knocking softly on her door.

"Yeah," she mumbled. "Come in."

She had the blinds pulled shut so I turned on the light.

"You, okay?" I asked her.

She smiled, lazily. "Yeah, just tired."

I sat down next to her on the bed. "You know, you really need to cool it on the wine, mom. The sheriff is going to think you're some kind of lush. You never usually drink like this."

"I didn't drink anything last night. At least, I don't remember," she said with a confused look.

"Oh, come on… mom, you were trashed. I had to help you to bed last night. You *had* to have been drinking."

She rubbed a hand over her forehead. "I don't even remember."

I sighed and changed the subject. "So, did his daughter make dinner for you?"

"I… think so."

My eyes widened. "You don't sound so sure."

She rubbed her forehead. "To tell you the truth, last night was a bit of a blur."

"I know the feeling," I said, staring towards her bedroom window. Last night almost felt like a dream. I couldn't explain my reaction to Ethan or the way he'd whisked me through the darkness the way he did. It didn't make a whole lot of sense.

"What?" she asked.

I turned back to her and smiled. "Nothing."

She stood up. "I've got so much to do today. I start work on Monday and have more errands than I have hours to complete them."

"*Ahem*, thanks for asking… my first day went pretty good, by the way."

115

"I'm sorry, honey," she replied, grabbing a robe from the closet. "I totally forgot. So, your first day at the diner went pretty smooth?"

"Yeah. I'm working again tonight. In fact, Nathan has to use your car to drop me off at the diner around four. His Mustang needs a new battery."

She groaned and then nodded reluctantly. "Okay. I'll just have to take care of some things tomorrow, I guess."

I motioned towards her neck. "So, how's your skin?" I asked.

She touched it and winced. "Still tender."

I got off the bed and walked over to her. "Did you put anything on it?"

"No. I probably should. How does it look?"

I examined her skin and frowned. It looked much worse. "You should really see a doctor."

She waved her hand and shook her head. "No, you know me. I'm just allergic to mosquito bites. It usually takes a while for them to heal."

"At least put something on it, so it doesn't get infected."

"Fine, Nurse Nikki," she said with a wry smile.

I walked over to the window and opened the blinds. "It's a beautiful day, mom, you could use some vitamin D on that lily-white skin of yours."

"Oh, hey... close the blinds," she gasped holding her hand up to shield her face. "The sun hurts my eyes!"

I quickly closed them. "Wow, you seriously need to lay off the alcohol, mom. Hangovers are a bitch."

She grabbed her sunglasses from the nightstand and put them on. "Actually, I think I have an eye infection or something," she said. "They've been bothering me the last couple of days."

"Maybe you're allergic to Caleb. Ever since you've been seeing him, you've been acting weird."

116

She smiled. "It's definitely not him. He is such a wonderful man. I'm so happy we met. It's only been a few hours since we we've been together, but... I have to admit, I miss him already."

It sounded like she really was falling pretty hard for the sheriff. "So, when's the wedding?" I asked.

'Oh, God, it's too early for that but I'll be honest, every time he looks at me," she sighed and her eyes looked wistful, "I just want to jump his bones."

I shuddered. "Okay, that's something I didn't need to hear. That's just twisted, mom."

She laughed. "Oh, just you wait, my dear. You'll meet someone who makes your toes curl and then you'll know exactly what I'm talking about."

I'd already met two guys who made my toes curl but I wasn't about to tell her that. "Whatever," I said.

She walked over to me and touched my cheek. "What about Duncan? Any sparks?"

My cheeks grew pink. "Well... I don't know. I mean, we're just friends, you know?"

She smiled, knowingly. "Friends, huh? Just make sure you use protection if he gets *too* friendly."

My jaw dropped. "Mom!"

"You are still a virgin, right?"

I couldn't believe we were actually having this conversation.

"Oh, my God, *yes!*" I replied, staring at her in horror.

"Although, you don't have to tell me if you don't want to. Just be safe."

"Enough! I'm still a virgin and I plan on staying one for a while."

Her eyes softened. "That's what a mother wants to hear. But when things get confusing or too much, you can always come to me with any questions."

"I'm going to take a shower," I said. "I feel dirty after talking about it with you."

She laughed. "You're such a smartass."

I left her and went back to my room. Instead of taking a shower, however, I lay down on my bed and thought about everything that had happened the night before. It now seemed so unbelievable, that I wondered if it had been just a dream. I closed my eyes and fell asleep.

~~~

"Nikki, come to me," whispered the smooth, masculine voice in my ear.

I opened my eyes to find that I was in a forest wearing a billowy, white nightgown. I stood up and began walking in my bare feet. As I looked down, I noticed sharp pieces of broken glass cutting into my skin, which was now bleeding.

"Hurry," prodded the voice. It was strong and demanding; it pushed me forward, one foot after another.

"Nikki!" yelled Duncan.

"Duncan?" I whispered, turning around.

"Wait, Nikki!" he cried, running towards me. I watched in amazement as he kept moving without making any progress.

There was a rush of movement and my heart began to race; I knew who it was. He'd come back for me. "Ethan?"

Someone grabbed my shoulders and started digging their sharp nails into my skin. I was shoved roughly to the ground and the shadow jumped on top of me. "Amy?" I whispered in horror.

Amy's eyes were filled with hate. "He's mine," she growled, her slit wrists bleeding onto my white dress. She opened her mouth and her pointy fangs closed in on my neck.

I opened my eyes and let out a shaky breath. Just a dream. Someone rapped on my door.

"Hey, twerp!"

"Yeah, come in," I mumbled, sitting up.

"Get ready," said Nathan. "I have to drop you off early at the diner. Mom needs the car as soon as I get back from purchasing a battery."

I looked at my alarm clock. It was already after two o'clock. "Okay," I said.

His eyes narrowed. "Are you doing okay?"

"Just a little tired."

He pointed at me. "Don't leave the diner after dark unless Duncan is with you."

"Yeah, okay."

He stared at me for a minute and then nodded. "Then, I'll be outside waiting for you. You have a half hour to get ready."

"Okay, I'll hurry."

I took a quick shower, put my uniform on, and spent a little extra time with my makeup. Then I pinned my damp hair up and stared into the mirror. I had to admit, I was definitely beginning to look more like my mother every day. I decided it was a good thing and smiled.

Nathan laid on the horn outside and I rushed out to meet him in mom's car.

"Makeup, huh? Trying to get more tips?" smiled Nathan.

I shrugged. "I could certainly use the money."

"I hear you. So, what do you think about last night? Pretty crazy, huh?"

"It was freaky, that's for sure. I still don't know what happened, exactly."

"I'm starting to think we really do have ghosts lurking around the cabin. That could be the real reason why mom's renting it so cheap."

"Makes sense."

We drove the rest of the way in silence and he dropped me off in front of the diner, warning me to stay put when my shift was over.

"You worry too much," I said. "I'm not going anywhere. I'll wait for Duncan."

"Here's Duncan's cell phone number," he said, handing me a slip of paper. "If there's a problem, call me or him."

"Okay, thanks."

When he finally drove off, I went into the diner and ran into Rosie in the back room.

"How's it going, Nikki?"

I smiled. "Pretty good. We were really swamped yesterday so Susan didn't get a chance to show me too much."

"Yeah, I heard. Since you're early, I'll go over some things with you, myself."

"Thanks."

Rosie went over the menus and showed me how to write up meal tickets. Then she gave me some pointers on how to juggle multiple tables and get them in and out as quickly as possible. When we were done, my head was spinning, but I felt like I was starting to get a little handle on things.

"Don't worry. It's going to take a while, but you'll get used to it. And, honey, don't be afraid to tell the customers you're new. They'll have more patience and might even tip you better."

"Oh, I'm all for that. Thanks."

"You'll do just fine here," she said, patting me on the shoulder. "Just do your best, and eventually things will fall together."

"Thanks, Rosie."

When Susan showed up, I shadowed her for half the day, and then I was given a couple of my own tables.

"You're doing great," said Rosie, after I served a large platter of food to one of my tables. "Keep it up."

"Thanks."

The time flew by quickly and by the time my shift was over, I'd made almost thirty dollars in tips. I was so giddy that I texted Nathan, who was happy for me.

"Listen, is there any way you can work a little later tonight?" asked Rosie, as I was about to punch out. "We could really use you until eleven o'clock. Darlene called in sick and I need all the help I can get. Since it's Friday night, we're going to get slammed soon."

"Okay. Let me call my ride and let him know. I'm sure it will be fine."

I grabbed my phone and called Duncan.

"Okay," he said, after I explained why they needed my help. "I'll be there promptly at eleven, though I'll expect a tip."

I giggled. "I think I can manage that."

We had a rush of customers around nine o'clock, and I was running ragged, trying to keep my orders right and not piss anyone off. By the time it was ten-thirty, I heaved a sigh of relief; the diner was finally clearing out.

"We usually get another big rush after the bars close," said Susan. "Just be thankful you're not working those customers. When they're not trying to pick you up, they're puking in the corner. It's really disgusting."

I grimaced. "I bet."

"Funny thing is, they usually tip better," she said, "because they're drunk and feeling extra generous. But, to me, it isn't really worth it."

Thinking about my mom last night and practically having to babysit her, I agreed. I then took out my tips and started counting it when Susan swore.

"What?" I said, looking up.

It was Ethan, followed by his clan. His eyes met mine and he smiled.

"Hey," whispered Susan, noticing the exchange. "Do you know him?"

"Um, not really," I said.

"Looks like they're in your section tonight, Nikki," said Rosie, "they usually only order coffee, though, so it should be a piece of cake."

I took a deep breath and walked up to their table.

"Hello," I said, handing out menus. "Can I start anyone out with something to drink?"

Ethan put his elbows on the table, clasped his fingers, and rested his chin on there. "Coffee for all of us, please, Nikki."

Remembering the effect he had on me, I averted my eyes. "And will you want food, or should I take away the menus?"

"Well," chuckled Ethan. "What I want probably isn't on the menu."

Oh, my God.

Our eyes met and I swear I could feel a charge of static electricity between us. It was eerie.

"You look beautiful tonight. As usual," he said softly.

The carnal promises he held in his smoldering eyes were raw and made my heart race. I took a step backwards, trying to catch my breath.

"Everything okay here?" interrupted Rosie, coming towards us.

Ethan looked away and I grabbed the back of an empty chair to steady myself.

"Yeah, Rosie," smiled Ethan. "Just being friendly with the new waitress."

She smiled. "Now don't be giving young Nikki here a hard time. It's only her second day."

For some reason, Rosie wasn't affected by Ethan's magnetic stare.

"Oh, don't worry about Nikki, Rosie. She's in good hands with me."

"That's what I'm afraid of," she chuckled. "So, Nikki, why don't you go pour some coffee for these boys."

I cleared my throat. "Okay,"

I grabbed six coffee cups and glanced towards Ethan's minions. I watched, curiously, as Rosie continued talking to Ethan while the rest of the guys seemed content just listening to the exchange, never actually joining in on the conversation. All were tall, pale, and rivaled any of the male models I'd seen in magazines. None of them compared to Ethan, however. His animal magnetism was enough to make me forget everything else.

"It's getting late," said Rosie, coming up to the counter. "Why don't you let me finish waiting on these guys and you can take off?"

I nodded, not quite trusting myself to talk.

Without another glance towards Ethan, I hurried to the break room, removed my apron, and grabbed my purse. When I turned around, I was staring into Ethan's eyes.

"Oh," I gasped.

"Leaving so soon?" he asked me, stepping closer. I moved backwards until my back hit the wall.

"I really have to go," I squeaked.

He touched my face and his eyes searched mine. "I've been searching for so long. I can't believe that I've finally found you."

My eyes widened. "Excuse me? I don't understand what you mean."

"You will." He closed his eyes and inhaled. "You smell so sweet."

I was so confused; my head was spinning and my stomach whirled. "I... what's happening?"

Ethan opened his eyes again and smiled. "You'll understand... in time."

Suddenly his mouth was on mine again, and as before, I couldn't resist his kisses. Our lips moved hungrily together and I moaned in pleasure, wanting him closer. I ran my hands up his back and into his hair, pulling his mouth harder against mine. But then he stopped abruptly and pulled away.

"I… I have to go and take care of something," he said thickly.

"Your eyes…" I whispered. They were still blue but glowed brightly with something that reminded me of fire.

He backed away from me, breathing heavily. "Leave your balcony door open tonight."

Then in a flash he was gone and I was left feeling frustrated.

Chapter Seventeen

"Nikki," said Rosie, stepping into the break room. "Someone named Duncan is waiting for you in the diner."

"Thanks."

Her eyes narrowed. "You okay? You look kind of flushed."

"I'm fine," I replied, not able to meet her eyes.

"Go home and get a good night's sleep," she said. "Working here can take a lot out of you."

"I will. Thanks."

I followed her back out and expected to see Ethan and his friends, but they were all gone.

"Hi," said Duncan.

He was dressed in a light blue polo shirt that complimented his silvery-gray eyes and low-riding jeans that showed off his tight abs. Because I was still feeling the pheromones from whatever Ethan produced, I had an incredible urge to jump his bones.

"Ready?" I asked, grabbing his hand.

He chuckled as I pulled him out of the diner. "What's wrong? Had enough of this place already?"

I released a heavy sigh and nodded. "It was a long day."

We both hopped in to his truck and he turned on the music. He caught me staring at him and smiled.

"You look nice," he said, grabbing my hand.

His smile was much more boyish than Ethan's and the tenderness in his eyes was so sweet. Part of me was already falling hard for Duncan, while another part of me screamed out for Ethan. It was frustrating and I decided to try and drive away my lustful thoughts of Ethan, so I told him to pull over to the side of the road.

"What's wrong?" he asked.

I scooted closer to him and pressed my lips against his. Soon we were kissing and my hands were all over him. When I pulled myself onto his lap and looked into his eyes, he let out a shaky sigh. "Nikki," he groaned, and then his mouth captured mine.

I ground my hips into his and he moaned with pleasure as I rocked against him. He unbuttoned the top of my uniform and raised my bra, kissing my breasts. Nobody had ever done that before and the sensation made me quiver down below.

"Shit," he groaned as a squad car pulled up behind us and we were surrounded by bright flashing lights.

I jumped off of him and buttoned my uniform while Duncan tried to compose himself. "Man," he said, looking at me again. "That was intense."

There was a tap on the window and we both smiled sheepishly at Sheriff Caleb, who was frowning.

"What's going on?" he asked.

Duncan's face looked so guilty it was comical. "Um, we were just talking."

126

He smirked. "You certainly fogged up the windows pretty good with all that talking you must have been doing. Next time, open one up."

We both smiled.

"Listen," said Caleb. "I'm not stupid, so I know your raging hormones probably got the better of you. Next time you feel like making out, though, don't do it on the side of the road. It's pretty dangerous, especially at night. Now, Duncan, bring Nikki home before her mom gets worried."

"Okay. Thank you, sir," answered Duncan.

He looked at me. "Say hello to your mother for me."

"Okay."

He walked back to his squad car, and we drove to the cabin in an awkward silence. Thankfully, Nathan was waiting on the porch for us when we pulled up because I didn't want to talk about what had just happened. The truth was, I wasn't exactly sure myself. That promiscuous girl back there? That wasn't me. I'd made out with two guys in the last two days and had no real explanation for it.

"Hey, guys," said Nathan, who was sitting on a gliding bench with a grim smile.

Duncan cleared his throat. "What's up, Nathan?"

"Read this," he said, holding out a newspaper.

I grabbed it from him and we both started reading the article he'd circled. There were several pictures of girls who were either missing or dead under the headline: 'Serial Killer Targeting Similar Victims?'

"They've included a picture of the girl who was found in the lake, as well as Amy," said Nathan, pointing. "See the resemblance there of the two girls?"

"Why is Amy included in this? She killed herself," I said.

Nathan's eyes narrowed. "Or maybe it *was* only made to look like she did. The most disturbing thing about this article is the photos of the girls."

"They look very similar," said Duncan. Then he turned to me and tensed up. "In fact, they look similar to Nikki, too."

My brother nodded. "Their hair is different but, if you look closely at the facial features of those girls, there is a definite resemblance to Nikki's. What really concerns me, are the strange things that have been happening to her. What if it's somehow related?"

"Seriously, I doubt it has anything to do with what's happened to all of those girls," I said.

"Still, we'd better keep a close eye on you," replied Nathan.

"Fine," I said, yawning. "Listen, I hate to be a party pooper, but I'm exhausted from being on my feet for the last several hours. I'm going to take a bath and then sleep for days, if mom will let me."

"Do you need any help getting that bath ready?" asked Duncan, smiling.

"Dude, that's my sister you're talking about. Don't say that stuff loud enough for my ears to pick up," said Nathan, looking horrified.

Duncan laughed.

"So, Duncan, are you planning on going to the barbeque tomorrow night?" I asked.

"Only if you're going," he said, leaning up against the cabin.

I smiled up at him. "Definitely. "

"How about if Nikki and I just meet you there?" interrupted Nathan. "I'll call you tomorrow afternoon."

"Sounds good," he replied.

"Goodnight Dunc," he said, opening the cabin door. "I'll give you guys some privacy, in case you want to suck face or something."

"Funny," I mumbled.

"Night," replied Duncan. As soon as Nathan was gone, he stepped closer and stared down into my eyes. "Well, goodnight."

"Goodnight.

He gave me one of his dimpled smiles and then leaned forward, kissing me tenderly on the lips. This time the kiss was short and sweet.

"Maybe tomorrow I won't smell like a diner," I said softly as he stepped back.

"Believe me," he replied, licking his lips. "I didn't mind one bit."

I cleared my throat. "I guess I'll see you tomorrow then?"

He reached into his pocket, pulled out his keys, and began twirling them around his finger. "Definitely. Can't wait."

"Me, too.

He motioned towards the door. "I'm not leaving until you're safely inside of the house."

His concern made me tingle. "Okay. Night."

"Goodnight."

I went inside the cabin and locked the door. When I turned around, Nathan stepped out of the kitchen with a bowl of popcorn.

"Where's mom?"

"Where else? Sleeping," he said, sitting down on the couch.

"Okay, I'm beat, too. I'll see you in the morning."

He nodded and flipped on the television.

I checked on mom and found her sprawled out on the bed, snoring softly. I closed the door and went into my room to get ready for my bath. I took out my hair down and set my cellphone on the charger, my head still spinning from everything that happened tonight. The fact that I'd made out with two guys in less than an hour was almost comical for someone like me; I still wasn't sure what to make of it. In California, I'd shied away from the opposite sex; here, I was totally acting like a slut.

Maybe it's the fresh air? I mused.

With a yawn, I walked into the bathroom and started the water. My cell phone began to ring and I rushed back into the bedroom to answer it. When I saw who it was, I sat down on the edge of my bed and smiled.

"I just wanted to say goodnight, again," said Duncan, a smile in his voice. "I... um, miss you already."

I laughed. "You'll be seeing me soon enough."

"Believe me, it won't be."

My heart melted. He was the sweetest guy and I told him so.

"You must bring it out in me," he replied. "Because, normally, I'm not like this."

"Really? That's hard to believe because you're a natural. I can just tell."

"Maybe, but I still think it's you." He sighed. "Look, this isn't easy for me, so I'm just going say it. I... I think I'm falling in love with you. Actually," he paused. "I know I am."

"You hardly know me," I said softly, although his words made me giddy. I'd never heard anyone says those words to me and it gave me tingles of pleasure.

"I know. Kind of weird, huh?"

I lay back on the bed and stared at the ceiling, a wide grin on my face. "No. I, um... actually, I think I'm falling for you, too."

"Really?"

He was sweet and made my stomach flutter. I'd never been in love before, but I knew one thing, I felt something special for him. I wasn't sure if it was love, but it sure felt good.

"Yeah, really."

"Okay, I just wanted you to know that I can't stop thinking about you, and it's driving me crazy."

"Was that before or after I attacked you in the truck?"

He chuckled. "Both."

I burst out laughing.

"Can I pick you up every night?" he teased. "I figure we'll be at third base if this keeps up."

"Oh, my God," I said. "Just for that, I'm sending you back to first base."

"I'll take what I can get. We don't even have to play the bases; we can just wander the fields."

I laughed again, and it reminded me of my mother with Caleb. *I was as pathetic as she was with men.*

"Man, I love your laugh."

My face hurt now, I was grinning so wide. "Thanks."

"No problem."

We sat in silence for a few seconds and then I spoke. "It's late and I was just about ready to take a bath."

He sucked in his breath. "I'll be right over."

"Duncan! I'm hanging up."

"Wait, are you naked yet?"

I groaned. "Goodnight, Duncan,"

"Just give me *something* to fantasize about."

I looked down at the uniform I was still wearing. "Yeah, I'm *totally* naked, except for the nail polish on my feet."

He groaned. "You're killing me."

"Night," I said. "This time… for real."

"Night," he murmured back.

He waited for me to hang up and I smiled again as I ended the call. One thing was for certain, Duncan was definitely the guy making my toes curl. No doubt about it.

I put my phone back in the charger, eyeing the balcony, suspiciously. The moon was bright, and normally I would have thought it was cool, but right now it was only ominous. There was no way that I was going to unlock the door, even if Ethan could somehow make it up here.

Ethan.

I didn't even know him and the conscious side of me knew that my reaction to the guy made no sense. Sure, I'd basically climbed all over him in our break room and his kisses ignited a raging fire inside of me, but the truth was, he scared the crap out of me, crazy sexy or not.

I checked the lock on the balcony door to make sure it was secure, then went back into the bathroom and got undressed. Seconds later, I had the jet streams going in the tub and my back was getting a much-needed water massage. I closed my eyes and soon began drifting off.

A strange noise jolted me awake, and I looked towards the window, only to find myself alone.

Must have been dreaming...

Sighing with relief, I checked the time and noticed I'd been in the tub for a half hour. The water was too chilly to enjoy anymore so I decided to get out. I toweled myself dry, put my robe on, and unplugged the bathtub. I then padded into the bedroom where I stopped dead in my tracks. Ethan was on my balcony, leaning against the railing watching me. He reminded me of a predator studying its kill before striking.

Time seemed to stand still as the realization of what Ethan really was sunk in. Obviously, he'd made it up to my balcony all by himself, and yesterday, we'd soared through the night faster than what was humanly possible. There could only be one explanation now, and it chilled me to the bone.

We stared at each other for what seemed like forever and then he pointed to the door.

Swallowing hard, I stepped over and unlocked it.

"Aren't you going to invite me in?" he asked softly.

My heart was hammering in my chest and I bit the side of my lip, trying to decide what to do.

"Well?" he asked, smiling devilishly. "I promise I won't hurt you, Nikki. In fact, I imagine you'll enjoy my company tremendously."

I let out a ragged sigh and nodded.

He stared at my mouth. "I'd like to hear you say it."

"Come in, Ethan."

Chapter Eighteen

Ethan stepped into my bedroom and I instinctively took a step backwards.

"Are you afraid of me?" he asked with a sardonic grin.

"I… don't know," I whispered, as the hair stood up on the back of my neck. Obviously I was lying. He scared the hell out of me.

He took another step towards me, his eyes probing. "Nikki, seriously, you have nothing to be afraid of."

"Uh, why me?" I squeaked, surprised that I was able to ask any questions at all when what I really wanted to do was run like hell.

Ethan's lips curled up. "Why not you?"

"I…" I stared at him as my panic began to change into something else entirely – an achy need to be closer to him; to touch and be touched by him.

What is wrong with me?

He walked over to my bed and sat down. "Come here."

I moved towards him and he grabbed both of my hands, kissing them with his soft lips.

"Why you? Because we belong together," he murmured.

Earlier his skin had felt cool to the touch. It had been the one thing that had surprised me. Now, his cheeks were warm and he held my hands against them, nuzzling them, lovingly.

"But I don't even know you," I said. "How can you say that?"

He shrugged. "You do. You just don't remember."

"That doesn't make sense. I just moved here," I said.

He looked up into my eyes. "Let's just say we knew each other in another life."

My eyes widened. "What… like reincarnation?"

His hands tightened on my wrists and he pulled me onto his lap. "Something like that."

"Seriously?"

Instead of answering me, he leaned forward and captured my lips with his. I closed my eyes, abandoning all logic and caution. Soon we were kissing with as much heat and passion as earlier, this time without fear of being interrupted. When his fingers opened up my robe and began touching my naked body, I gasped with pleasure.

"Ethan," I breathed, my heart pounding in my chest.

"You're mine," he whispered into my neck, making me shiver. "Forever."

"Sure," I whispered back as his tongue slid down to my nipple and began teasing it. "Whatever… you… say."

His hands caressed my breasts and I closed my eyes as his hot mouth continued to make me quiver. Soon, I was making mewling noises and he was breathing as heavily as I was.

"What?" I whispered when he suddenly pushed me away.

"Come with me," he said in a ragged voice. "I can't make love to you here. It's not safe."

135

"No, it's okay. Nobody will know," I whispered, surprising myself with my own eagerness to give myself to him.

He closed his eyes. "You're a virgin and I'm..."

How did he know? Obviously, not from my actions.

"What? It's okay."

"Come with me now, Miranda," he said, opening his eyes and pulling me to him. "It's time to leave everything else, behind."

I pulled away. "Miranda?"

He blinked. "Nikki, come with me and we can be together forever. I'll never let you go, again."

"What? I can't leave my family," I said. Sure, he was hot and I wanted to feel him touch and kiss me again, but I wasn't about to leave my family.

He stared into my eyes, and soon I was willing to go anywhere with him. I just wanted nothing more than to be lost in his arms forever. "Come with me," he prodded, touching my face, lovingly.

I nodded. "Oh, God. Yes."

Just then the bedroom door was thrown open and my brother stood in the doorway with a shotgun. "Hands off of her, pal. She's not going anywhere with you!"

Ethan growled and moved away from me as I struggled to adjust my robe.

"Did you just *growl* at me? Get the hell out of here, Cujo, before I use this thing!" demanded Nathan. "I'll fucking do it!"

Ethan took a step towards my brother and I yelled, "Ethan, don't hurt him! Please!"

Somehow deep down, I knew that Ethan had the power to rip Nathan apart with little effort. Even though both of them were similar in size and stature, you could almost feel the power and strength emanating from him. It was both frightening and exciting at the same time. At least for me.

Ethan looked at me and for a second, I thought he was going to carry me off into the moonlight. Instead, he let out a frustrated groan, and then in a flash, was gone.

"*What* in the hell was that?" hollered Nathan as he dashed towards the balcony.

"Um, that was Ethan," I answered, touching my bruised lips. I couldn't believe how much I wanted him to return. To finish what he'd started.

Nathan stormed back into my bedroom and ran a hand through his brown hair. "What were you thinking, Nik? That has to be the *thing* trying to fuck with us. That certainly wasn't a normal dude who was trying to feel you up, which, by the way, wasn't at all fair to Duncan!"

A wave of shame spread through me as Duncan's face popped into my mind. I did love him, didn't I?

"Listen," I said firmly. "He has this power to make me do things… I can't control myself around him," I shook my head incredulously. "Nathan, God, I seriously think I'd do anything for him if he asked."

"What?"

"I know," I said, my eyes misting over. "I couldn't help it, either. One moment I was fine and the next, we were making out and I did nothing to stop it."

His eyes narrowed. "Mind control?"

I wiped a tear from my eye, my emotions all messed up. "Yes."

"So, do you honestly believe he's a vampire?"

"Yes, Nathan, I do." My mind was beginning to clear, and now there was little doubt in my mind that he actually was a vampire.

He leaned forward. "Did he suck your blood or anything?"

I touched my neck. "He didn't bite me. At least… not that I remember." I ran over to the mirror and checked my neck.

"See, it looks normal." Remembering our mother's neck, I covered my mouth in horror. "Oh, my God... mom! She has that thing on her neck! Remember?"

We both flew out of the bedroom and began knocking on her door.

"Come in," she called.

Her room was dark except for a candle burning slowly on the nightstand.

"Hey," I said, in a low voice. "Um, sorry to bother you. We were just wondering if we could check those bites on your neck. To make sure they aren't infected."

She rolled over and gave us an exasperated sigh. "You woke me up in the middle of the night to check my neck?"

"Sorry," said Nathan. "Um, we saw this news report about these mosquito bites that get really inflamed if you don't care for them correctly."

"Yeah," I said. "If you don't clean them good... um, eggs will grow in your neck."

She sat up and shrieked. "What?! Eggs! Look and see if anything is growing in my neck!"

Nathan bit back a smile as we stepped closer to examine mom's neck.

"Fine, I'm convinced," he whispered, looking at me. "Check it out."

I was, too. The swelling had gone down but the two holes could have definitely been caused by a vampire. Not that either of us were experts, but we'd watched enough horror flicks to know what we saw.

"Mom, we have to talk to you," I said, stepping back. "I know this is going to sound crazy but you have to believe us."

She looked at both of us. "Okay, spill it. What's on your minds?"

We started over from when we'd spoken to Amy, her warnings, and how she'd killed herself. Then, I told both of them how I met Ethan and how he'd called me Miranda and had almost made me run away with him.

She threw her head back and laughed.

"It's not funny, mom," said Nathan. "This Ethan guy looked like he was ready to attack me tonight and I had to use a gun to scare him away."

"Nathan, I doubt the gun would have killed him, anyway," I said. "He only left you alone because I told him to."

"Whatever," he snapped. "This guy is some kind of monster. Whether it's a vampire or demon. He flies, he growls – he isn't normal!"

She threw her hands up in the air. "It's… I don't know how to react to this. I can't just accept the fact that you both think this kid is a vampire. As far as my neck goes, I've never met Ethan, so if you think he bit my neck when I was having a cup of coffee and didn't notice, you have another thing coming."

"Do you feel different at all?" I asked.

She glared at me. "For Heaven's sake, Nikki! I'm not going to turn into a damn vampire!"

Nathan and I looked at each other. We knew it was pointless to keep trying to convince her that there were vampires in Shore Lake. Unless she saw it for herself, there was no way she was going to believe us. Nathan had reacted the same way.

She rubbed her temples and then stared at us, again. "Look, I'm going back to bed and I suggest that the both of you do the same thing. In the morning, you'll both realize how crazy this sounded."

I sighed. "Okay."

"Goodnight, mom," said Nathan.

"I love you both, but if you wake me up to talk about vampires again, I'm getting rid of cable!"

Chapter Nineteen

"Okay, I'm not leaving you alone anymore," said Nathan as he paced back and forth in the kitchen. We were both too shook up to sleep.

"Fine," I said, taking a sip of coffee.

He wagged his finger. "We should talk to mom and see if she's willing to move back home, too."

My jaw dropped. "But what about Duncan and our new jobs?"

"What about… there's a vampire after you, Nikki? Or should we call you *Miranda*?"

I sighed. "What if he follows us anyway? He said he's been looking for me and now that he's found me, we are supposed to be together."

"How romantic," snickered Nathan. "If you ask me, I think he just wants to get into your pants."

"He almost did," I mumbled.

"Good thing I heard those groans and whimpers coming from your room, which was gnarly, by the way. Do you know how disturbing it is to hear your sister getting it on with a vampire?" He shuddered. "It's sick."

I smiled. "Thank you for being a nosy brother, Nathan. You probably saved my life. At least, my virginity."

"Thank my stomach. If it wasn't for mom's leftover pasta salad calling to me in the fridge, we wouldn't be having this conversation."

"Probably not."

He sat down by the counter. "I just don't know what else to do. You know, I wonder if we should see if Abigail is still in town. She might have some ideas. She's the only other person who'd believe us."

"We should probably go and pay her a visit in the morning," I said.

He looked at his watch. "The sun will be up soon. I'm going to grab my sleeping bag and camp out in your room for the next few nights. Hopefully, that horny vampire gives up and decides to go after someone else."

"Oh, my God," I whispered in horror. "What if he killed all of those girls in the paper? You said they were all similar looking. Maybe he was looking for me?"

He snorted. "Or worse yet, you are not the real Miranda and he decides to kill you when he figures it out."

I glared at him. "Oh, thanks, Nathan. Just when I think it can't get any worse."

"Hey, I'm just trying to keep everything in perspective. I mean, we shouldn't rule anything out," he said with a yawn.

His yawn triggered one from me. "True, but I hope you're wrong," I said as we headed out of the kitchen and back upstairs.

Ten minutes later, Nathan was snoring on the floor but I was still awake. I stared at the door to my balcony, which was now closed and locked. Part of me still longed for Ethan and I wondered if I'd have the strength to say no if given the chance to surrender to him again.

Chapter Twenty

"Wake up, Princess of Darkness," teased my brother the next morning.

"Very funny," I mumbled. I looked at my alarm clock to find it was already after eleven o'clock.

"I talked to Duncan already," said Nathan, between bites of a banana. "We're supposed to meet him at the marina around four o'clock."

I yawned. "Did you tell him about last night?"

"I told him some things but left out the part where you were sitting on Ethan's lap, panting away."

I groaned. "It was pretty bad. I'm so disgusted with myself."

"You were certainly enjoying it last night." He grimaced. "Heck, I was the one disgusted."

"Come on, you know very well that it wasn't me, last night. Aren't I typically the frigid and shy twin?"

His lips curled up. "True. I'm usually the one fighting off the opposite sex."

I got out of bed. "I'm taking a shower now. At least you don't have to follow me everywhere during the day. Vampires don't like the daylight."

"As far as we know," he said. "But this is real life. I wouldn't count anything out."

"I've only run into Ethan at night. In fact, he usually hangs out at the diner after dark."

His eyes narrowed. "What in the hell does he order? Steak Tartare?"

I grimaced. "Gross, no, he only orders coffee; he and his five friends."

"Oh, hell, more vampires?"

"I think so, although the others never say a word. They just sip coffee and stare at the rest of the customers."

"Probably planning a strike."

"I wouldn't doubt it. Look, I'm taking a shower. I'll meet you downstairs in a little while. Is mom awake?"

His face darkened. "No, that's another thing that's still bothering me. This isn't like her, at all."

"I know. We'd better keep an eye on her. Maybe give the sheriff a heads-up, too," I said.

"He already thinks we're nuts," said Nathan. "Can you imagine if we tell him about last night?"

I bit my lower lip. The sheriff would *never* believe us. "Let's keep it to ourselves, for now."

"We're going to have to."

Nathan left my room and I took a hot shower. When I was done, I slipped on a white sundress and a pair of sandals. After I dried my hair and added a little makeup, I stared at the results and frowned. I definitely looked like I was going on a date.

I'm doing it solely for Duncan, I told myself.

"You getting dolled up for Duncan or trying to catch a vampire?" joked my brother when I stepped into the kitchen.

I scowled. "For your information, I am doing it for Duncan."

"Wow, you look very fresh and lovely this morning," said mom as she walked into the kitchen.

I smiled. "Thanks, mom. By the way, it's the afternoon, now."

She removed her sunglasses and looked at the clock. Her face fell. "Oh."

"Your eyes still bothering you?" I asked.

She nodded. "I have an eye appointment today. I was lucky to get one on a Saturday."

"I thought the entire town would be shut down with everything going on," replied Nathan.

"What do you mean?" she asked.

"The town barbeque thingy," I said. "We're meeting Duncan there later this afternoon. Want to join us, mom? It should be a lot of fun."

"Yeah, actually, I do." Her eyes lit up. "Maybe I'll see Caleb there."

"He's the sheriff. He's probably heading up the security," said Nathan.

"I'm sure. I'll probably just meet you both there after my eye appointment. Keep your cell phone on so I can find you."

"Just call me when you're done and we'll come look for you, mom," said Nathan.

"Okay. This should be fun," she said, turning on the coffeemaker.

"Either of you want eggs?" asked Nathan, opening the fridge. "I don't know about you two, but I'm craving a late breakfast."

"No, that's okay," she replied, picking out one of her gourmet coffees from the carousel on the counter. "I'm hungry, but nothing sounds good. I think I'm just going to grab a bite in town before my exam."

144

Nathan and I looked at each other, both of us obviously wondering the same thing, *was she craving something rare and bloody?*

"Nikki, are you hungry?" asked mom.

"Uh, just some toast."

"Okay."

Mom made some for me and then took off with her coffee, while Nathan made himself a monster omelet. After watching him down a half dozen eggs while I nibbled on my toast and jelly, we decided to take a drive over to Abigail's, to see if she was still in town.

"I think this is her place," he said as we drove up the dirt road to the next cabin over. It was older and much smaller than the one we were staying at, but kept up nicely. With all of the flowers and shrubs surrounding the cabin, it seemed inviting.

"Yeah, there's her truck," I pointed next to the cabin. "Obviously she didn't skip town just yet. Lucky for us."

We got out and walked up to the porch. I could hear a dog barking somewhere inside and smiled. "At least we know she's not living alone."

"I don't blame her," said Nathan, swatting at a mosquito. "Not with Ethan and his band of freaks flying around at night. Hell, maybe we should consider getting a dog."

"Something tells me a dog isn't going to frighten a vampire," I said. "If anything, it might put the dog's life in grave danger."

"No doubt," he replied, ringing the doorbell. We waited and rang it again, but nobody answered.

"Maybe she's fishing on the dock?" I asked.

He stared over my head towards the side of the cabin and nodded. "Good thinking. Let's go check it out."

We went around to the back and looked out towards the lake, but there was still no sign of anyone.

I looked up at Nathan and frowned. "You know, I'm getting this creepy feeling, that something isn't right."

"Don't get all paranoid, Nik. She's probably taking a walk or over at a friend's nearby."

"Yeah. Let's hope so."

We walked to the back door, and this time, I pounded on it. When nobody answered, I looked through a small kitchen window and saw a dog sitting inside in a kennel, whining.

"Aw… poor thing. She's got her Golden Retriever caged up. Maybe Abigail really is getting ready to leave town, today."

He scraped his teeth over his lower lip and nodded. "Makes sense. Heck, I'm surprised she's still here."

"Let's wait on the porch for a little while," I said, walking towards the front of the cabin again. "If she is heading out, we need to catch her beforehand."

We both sat down on the wooden rockers on the porch and stared pensively towards the dirt road. After about fifteen minutes, I glanced back at her empty truck and sighed. "Something isn't right, Nathan. I just have this horrible, horrible feeling."

He stood up. "I know. I'm wigging out a little here, myself. You know, she's pretty old. What if she had a stroke or heart attack, and is lying inside, unable to move?"

I rose to my feet, too. "Oh crap. Check the door."

Nathan reached for the handle, and it opened easily. He stuck his head inside. "Hello? Abigail? It's Nathan from the next cabin over!"

Nobody answered.

"Keep going," I said.

We stepped inside and were immediately engulfed in a smell that made me want to puke.

"What's that smell?" I whispered in horror, stopping in my tracks. It was worse than garbage that's been baking in the sun and dog shit – combined.

"Oh, hell, I don't know. Let's go find her bedroom," he mumbled, his hand over his nose. "Just stay behind me."

We searched the cabin until we found a room that appeared to be her bedroom. On the full-sized bed were two open suitcases and piles of women's clothing, ready to be packed.

I looked at Nathan. "What now?"

"Kitchen."

I followed him out of the bedroom and we both gasped in horror the moment we entered the kitchen. On the floor, next to the refrigerator, lay Abigail – her neck ripped open and her lifeless eyes fixed on the ceiling. We both shrieked and then ran like hell out of the cabin, back to his Mustang.

"Oh, my God, we have to call the cops!" I cried. "That was horrible!"

"Did you see her eyes?" he choked, his face whiter than my dress. He pulled his phone out and dialed nine-one-one. After he hung up with the police, he started the engine.

Dizzy and afraid of puking, I opened my window to let some fresh air in. "I guess there's no question that vampires are involved, now, is there?"

"Hell no. Let's get out of here and call mom when we get back to the cabin. The police told me to stick around, but screw that. They know where to find us."

"I agree."

He kicked up rocks as we peeled out of the driveway and I closed my eyes, trying to get the image of Abigail's body out of my head. If Ethan was responsible for that, there was no way in hell I'd want to see him again. As far as I was concerned, it was time to talk mom into leaving town.

Chapter Twenty-One

A squad car stopped by our cabin an hour later, asked us several questions, and then left. Because we didn't want to sound crazy, we didn't mention a word about vampires.

"That must have been so horrifying," said mom, who'd stopped back home after we'd called to let her know what had happened.

"Her throat was torn apart, mom," said Nathan. "There was blood everywhere. It was just... crazy."

Sighing, she picked off a piece of lint from her jean skirt. "Maybe it was a bear or a mountain lion that attacked her."

Nathan's face darkened. "Or maybe it was a vampire."

She groaned. "You're not going to start with that business, again, are you?"

He sighed. "Look, you know us. We aren't making it up, mom. This Ethan dude, he literally flew out of Nikki's room."

"He'd better think twice before he sneaks into your sister's bedroom, again."

He smiled grimly. "Mom, if we aren't careful, they'll be bloodsucking lovers for the rest of eternity. No lie."

Mom burst out laughing. "You're so melodramatic."

I knew she still wouldn't believe the vampire story, and part of me didn't blame her. I was still having a hard time accepting it, myself.

"Listen," she said, looking down at her watch. "I'm going to be late for my eye appointment if I don't leave. Are you both still going to this town barbeque?"

Nathan and I looked at each other.

"We should," I told him. "Duncan's expecting us and I'm afraid that Ethan is coming back later. He might hurt you."

"Nikki, if you think someone is going to hurt your brother, then you call the police right away!" snapped mom. "I mean, seriously!"

"Mom," said Nathan. "The police can't stop this guy."

She rubbed her forehead. "Well, we'll talk about this later. I'll see you at in town. Have your cell phones on you."

After mom left us, I called Duncan and told him about finding Abigail.

"No shit? I wonder if Ethan was responsible for killing her."

"I don't know. I mean, he didn't actually seem like a killer to me."

Duncan paused. "Even so, if I catch that guy anywhere around you, I'm going to pound his head in."

I smiled. "You'd do that for me?"

"Damn right," he replied. "As far as I'm concerned, you're *my* girl now."

"I like that sound of that," I replied, softly.

"Oh, hell, my dad's calling me. Look, I'll see you guys around four o'clock. Call me if you have any problems. I can't *wait* to see you. I thought about you all night."

"Me too," I replied, although I'd been thinking about how I'd pretty much cheated on him, even though I'd been a

149

victim myself. I only hoped that he wouldn't find out about it. He was such a sweet guy and didn't deserve to be hurt.

As I hung up, Nathan walked out of the kitchen with some garlic and told me to try and find the cross necklace that my father had given me.

"I lost it," I said with a grim smile, "last summer."

He sighed. "You know, I never thought I'd meet someone more dangerous to us than our dad."

"We don't know for sure if Ethan killed our neighbor or those girls."

Nathan scowled. "Don't start making excuses for this...thing."

"He has friends. Maybe one of them killed Abigail?"

"Just stop, okay? Ethan is no good for you. If he has killed people, then you have to stay away from him."

"I know," I said.

"Rub some of this garlic on your wrists," he said, holding it out.

I backed away. "Yeah, right. I'm not going to walk around smelling like pizza, especially walking through crowds of people."

He shrugged. "Fine then, let's just go."

Twenty minutes later, we arrived in town and parked at the marina. Duncan was waiting for us in the shop.

"Hey, Duncan," said Nathan.

"Hey, Nathan."

Duncan walked over and put his arms around me. "Are you okay?"

I nodded.

He tilted my chin up and stared into my eyes. "I'm not leaving your side anymore. Not until this guy is behind bars. Or... whatever the hell he is."

I nodded.

"Wow, you look... beautiful," he said. "I'd better keep my eyes on you." Then he brushed my lips with his.

"Let's get going, I'm starving," interrupted Nathan.

Duncan smiled and put his arm around my shoulders as we started walking towards the town festival.

"Wow, they really go all out," said Nathan.

Large tents and carnival rides were set up in the park and the smell of succulent barbequed meat and corndogs drifted through the air. Crowds of people were already stuffing their faces, standing in line for the rides, or chasing after their kids.

Nathan groaned. "I'm starving, lead me to the chow."

A half hour later we were sitting at a picnic table watching Nathan devour his second helping of ribs and listening to some band play old time rock-n-roll songs. Nathan's cell phone began to ring. He licked his fingers and answered the phone.

"Mom's on her way," he said after hanging up.

"Nikki!"

I looked up and saw Susan walking over. I introduced her to Nathan and Duncan.

"I thought you had to work today?" I asked her.

"No. They closed down for the day because of the festival, thank goodness," she answered.

"Did you eat yet?" asked Nathan, sliding over to make room for her at the picnic table.

She shook her head. "No, but that's okay. I'm going to get something later."

"You can sit down with us. I don't bite," he said, his lips curling up. "Unless you want me to."

Susan blushed and sat down next to him.

I smiled in amusement as Nathan began teasing her some more. Susan looked totally different out of uniform and reminded me a little of a younger Jennifer Aniston. My brother must have liked what he saw, because he was totally laying on the charm.

"So, do you know this Ethan character?" asked Nathan after a while.

"I only know that he pursued Amy and she had this notion he was a vampire."

"Did she say why she thought he was a vampire?" asked Duncan.

She shrugged. "Just that he only came out at night and had this power to make her do whatever he wanted. It freaked the hell out of her."

"So, did he ever try hitting on you?" asked Nathan.

She stared at her clasped fingers. "No, but I went out with one of his friends a couple of times."

My eyes widened. "You went out with one of the guys he comes in with at night?"

"Not one of them. I went out with Drake, who was more of a loner. Then, he kind of just fell off of the face of the earth. He used to come in at night alone and we'd go out after my shift. Then one night, he just never came back. I tried calling him but he never even returned my calls."

"Did you really think he was a vampire?" I asked.

She shook her head. "No. I mean he was kind of intense and kept weird hours, but of course he wasn't a vampire. There's no such thing, right?"

Nathan and I stared at each other, but didn't respond.

"Did you ever go to his house?" asked Duncan.

"We stopped by once, but he made me wait outside. He lived with Ethan and the others; they rent this house on the edge of town."

"You didn't think it was weird that he made you wait outside?" I asked.

She shook her head. "Not really. Besides, Ethan and the others really creep me out. Drake was different, though. I wish I knew what happened to him."

"Did you ask Ethan?" I said.

She made a face. "Yeah but he didn't say much. Personally, I think he went back home to Australia. He talked about his family a lot and how he missed them."

My eyebrows shot up. "He was Australian?"

She nodded and got this dreamy look on her face. "Yeah, he had this neat accent. Man, I miss that guy."

Duncan cleared his throat. "So you know where Ethan lives?"

"Yes."

"Maybe we should call the sheriff and tell him we think Ethan's responsible for those murders?" said Nathan.

Susan's jaw dropped. "You seriously think that Ethan is responsible?"

"We don't know for sure," I said.

Nathan scowled. "As far as I'm concerned, he's responsible for something."

Embarrassed, I looked away. I'd let Ethan into my bedroom and allowed him to do those things to me. What was even worse was that I'd enjoyed it, and wasn't even certain that I had regrets.

Was he a murderer?

I didn't want to believe it.

"Here comes mom," said Nathan, standing up. He waved and she walked over.

"So, what did the eye doctor say?" I asked. She was still wearing her sunglasses.

She shrugged. "He prescribed some eye drops for me. He thinks it might be an eye infection, but doesn't know for sure. If the drops don't work then I'm supposed to come back in five days for more tests."

"Hopefully you won't have to wear your sunglasses to work on Monday."

She smiled. "Now *that* would be awkward, wouldn't it? So," she looked around. "Have you seen Caleb, yet?"

I shook my head. "No. Did you call him?"

"I did, but he never answers during the day. He says it's because he's so busy. I just hope it's not something else."

"Like what? Another woman?" I asked.

She smiled, sheepishly. "Yeah, maybe."

"Are you talking about Sheriff Caleb?" asked Susan.

"Yeah," I said.

"He's definitely not married," she said. "He has a daughter who just graduated, Celeste. His wife died a few years ago."

"That's what he told me, too," said mom.

"So what's the sheriff's daughter like?" I asked.

"Oh, I forgot to tell you! The redhead we saw on our first day in town… the cute one? *That's* Celeste."

"The hot one?" asked Nathan.

"Yes, Nathan. 'The hot one'," she said with a smile.

Nathan turned to Susan. "No offense, Susan. You're really hot, too."

Susan's cheeks turned bright red again.

"Hey, here comes my dad," said Duncan, waving his hand.

Sonny walked over with a plate of food and sat down next to mom. He smiled. "Hi, I'm Duncan's dad… you must be Nikki and Nathan's mom? I'm Sonny and I'm going to apologize right now for making a pig out of myself."

Mom laughed. "I'm Anne. That's quite all right. I'm used to it, Nathan eats round the clock."

"I have to be back at the marina in fifteen minutes so I have to eat fast."

I watched as my mom and Sonny began talking about some yacht he was currently fixing.

"How fascinating," she said. "I've always wanted a ride on a beautiful yacht."

He smiled. "Come on by the marina sometime and I'll take you out on a couple. I own a fifty-foot carver myself, and haven't had a chance to take it out much this summer. You'd give me a reason to start the engine.

My mom's face lit up. "That sounds wonderful."

"I'd better get back," he said, standing up. "It was nice meeting you, Anne. Susan, I'll see you at the diner again, I'm sure."

"See you, Mr. Hamilton," answered Susan.

"I probably won't be home until late," said Duncan.

Sonny's eyes narrowed. "That's right. Call me if you need me."

When Sonny left, mom smiled. "Your dad seems very nice, Duncan."

"Thanks."

She looked at me. "And cute, too."

I laughed. He *was* pretty hot for an older guy.

Nathan stood up. "Anybody interested in going on some rides? Susan?"

"Sure," she answered.

"Duncan, how about some rides?" I asked.

He nodded. "Let's go."

"I'm going to be taking off," said mom. "Caleb's supposed to be stopping over after work. I don't see him patrolling around here anyway."

There were a few cops wandering around but I hadn't seen Caleb around either.

"Okay, bye, mom," I said.

"Don't stay up too late," said Nathan.

"Same goes for you, *dad*," she replied.

We purchased some carnival tickets and then spent the next couple of hours screaming on the rides. I watched in amusement as Nathan pretended to be frightened and hugged Susan for comfort.

"They seem to be hitting it off," said Duncan as we got on the Ferris wheel by ourselves.

"Yeah."

Duncan's face darkened. "So, what exactly happened between you and Ethan?"

Chapter Twenty-Two

"Not much," I lied.

His eyes narrowed. "Nathan mentioned he was in your bedroom?"

"Yes. He knocked on the door and I opened it. I'm not even sure why I did. He has this way of manipulating people. You heard Susan."

"He'd better leave you alone or I'll manipulate his face," he said. He then put his arms around me and drew me close.

I smiled in pleasure as his lips closed in on mine. Within a matter of seconds, I'd forgotten all about Ethan and was kissing Duncan back as hungrily as he was kissing me. Then the ride was ending, and we were forced to pull apart

"What are you doing to me?" he murmured.

I'd certainly felt his excitement brush against me and decided it was probably better that the ride had ended when it did.

"So, Duncan, how many girls have you been with?'

He looked at me in surprise. "Is it important?"

"No, not really."

"If it makes you feel better, I've only been with one other girl. We went out for a few months when I was living with my mom, in Minnesota."

"Do you miss her?"

He grabbed my hand and squeezed it. "You're all I care about, Nikki. I've never felt this way about anyone."

I smiled and kissed him.

"What about you?" he asked, when I pulled away.

I blushed. "Actually, I'm a virgin."

He raised his eyebrows.

"What?"

"You are?"

I scowled. "Yeah, why? Do I seem easy to you or something."

He burst out laughing. "No! I'm sorry. You just know how to…"

I smiled wickedly. "Excite you? You're a guy. It's not too difficult to figure out."

"So, you're really a virgin?" he said, rubbing the bottom of his chin. "Hmm…I'd better be careful then. You're like a delicate flower that needs to be handled with kid gloves."

I snorted. "Yeah right!"

"Okay, maybe I should tell you to be careful with *me*."

"Maybe, you should."

He smiled as the Ferris wheel stopped at the ground and then helped me down.

"There's Nathan and Susan," I said, pointing towards the ticket booth. They were apparently going on more rides.

"Would you like to go on more rides?" he asked, pulling out his wallet.

"Actually, I have to use the ladies' room," I said, looking around.

He nodded. "I'll come with you."

We walked towards the beach where there was a public restroom open for the festival, which was good because I hated using the satellites.

"Do you want to take a walk by the beach?" he asked when I was finished.

I looked towards the beach. It was dusk and now deserted. "Sure."

We walked towards the lake and I took off my sandals so I could dig my toes in the sand.

"Now that I've got you alone…" he grinned, grabbing my arm and pulling me close.

Duncan was almost a foot taller than me and I stood on my tippy toes to meet his lips. We started kissing and then I remembered.

"Wait," I said. "It's getting dark. We shouldn't be out here alone."

He snorted. "Listen, if Ethan shows up, I'll knock his lights out."

Duncan would have been a formidable adversary for anyone, but not for whatever kind of creature Ethan was. There was no question in my mind about that.

"Duncan, he's not normal. Remember how he grabbed me and ran through the woods? Even you can't compete with that."

He sighed. "Fine. Just one more kiss and we'll head back."

I slid my arms around his neck and we began kissing, again. Just when my legs began to feel like jelly, he released me.

"Hey," I pouted as I opened my eyes.

"Well, well, well," chuckled Ethan. "You're a naughty little vixen, aren't you?"

Duncan lay on the ground, obviously unconscious. I rushed to his side and looked up at Ethan. "What did you do to him?!" I yelled.

He sighed. "Don't worry he's just taking a little nap. I *should* have killed him for even touching you."

"Ethan, you have to stop this. I'm not Miranda."

He grabbed my hand and lifted me up. "You are Miranda. I can see it in your eyes, the way you smell, how you taste…" he murmured, looking into my eyes.

My heart began to race as he bent his head and began kissing me. A wave of hot pleasure shot through my body and I released a strangled moan.

Just then, Duncan came back to his senses. "Leave her alone, you asshole!" he raged, trying to get Ethan away from me.

Ethan's eyes burned with fury and I watched in awe as he let out an unearthly roar. Before I could do anything, he held Duncan in the air by his throat.

"Please, stop!" I sobbed, rushing towards them. I started hitting Ethan in the back, but it was like hitting a plate of steel. He used his other hand and pushed me to the ground.

Duncan's eyes were bugging out of his head and his face was turning purple. I knew he would die if I didn't do something.

"Ethan!" I screamed, getting back up. I hit him repeatedly with my fists, but he continued to ignore me. It was only when a group of men began racing towards us that he swore and released Duncan.

"Let's go, now," ordered Ethan.

I backed away from him and then turned to run. Before I could take five steps, I was in his arms and we were racing across the beach like a flash of lightning.

"No…" I sobbed as the lights from the carnival became a blur.

Chapter Twenty-Three

I woke up in a cool, dark bedroom. Candles lit up the room and rock music played softly in the background.

I sat up. "Duncan?" I mumbled, "Nathan?"

Someone sighed and I found Ethan watching me from the shadows. He sat in a leather club chair that had been pushed into the corner of the room.

"So, you're finally awake," he murmured.

I swallowed. "Where am I?"

"Welcome to my humble abode," he chuckled. He was naked from the waist up and my mind turned traitor once again as I imagined running my fingers over his impressive pecs.

What in the hell was wrong with me?!

I forced my lustful thoughts aside and tried to concentrate on Duncan and whether or not he was safe.

"Take me home," I demanded, scooting to the edge of the bed. "Please."

His eyes studied me intently, but he didn't respond.

I stood up and smoothed down my dress. "Seriously, take me home," I said, lifting my chin.

Ethan stood up and walked towards me. His eyes lowered to my dress and I suddenly felt naked. I wondered if vampires had x-ray vision.

I put a hand to my chest and looked up at him. "Ethan?"

"You *are* home," he replied, his voice husky. I backed away and he grinned. "Are we playing hard to get, now?"

I ignored the question. "Look, this is insane. You can't just keep me here like a prisoner."

His eyes hardened. "Prisoner? If you want to leave, you're certainly free to go." He then stood sideways so that I could move around him to the doorway.

Holding my breath, I decided to go for it. Before I could take two steps, however, he grabbed both of my hands and had them behind my back before I had a chance to exhale.

"You know you want to be with me," he said, smiling darkly. "In every way."

I stared up into eyes that hinted of things I'd only fantasized about, and shamefully, my resistance fell apart.

Yes, I wanted Ethan...

In fact, from the tingling sensation growing between my legs, I wanted him every way and everywhere.

One of his large hands slid into my hair, cupping the back of my head. "Let me," he whispered seductively, his breath hinting of butterscotch once again, "please you."

Oh, my God...

My eyes lowered to his mouth and I licked my lips, remembering how good they'd felt on my skin. The next thing I knew, he had me on the bed, pressing against me, and I surrendered all control, gasping in guilty pleasure. Within seconds I was returning his kisses as passionately as he was giving them.

"Yes," he growled, against my mouth as my hands traveled along his back to his hair. I tightened my fingers around the strands and pulled him closer, kissing him deeper as hot waves of desire shot through my veins, urging me on.

More... I wanted more...

I wrapped my legs around his waist, this time holding him captive as our pelvises moved together in a rhythm that soon had me whimpering in pleasure.

Suddenly, he stopped and his body tensed up.

"What?" I asked, staring up at him.

He closed his eyes and his jaw tightened.

"What did I do?" I whispered, touching his cheek.

He opened his eyes and they seemed to burn right into my soul. I stared in awe as a fire ignited around his irises and grew into flames.

My eyes widened. "Are you okay?"

He touched my cheek with his finger, drawing circles. "I'm fine... and you've done nothing but... make me want you more than ever," he whispered. "I just needed a second to regain my control."

"Oh."

"Now, where were we?" he asked as his fingers moved down my neck and across my chest. Before I could respond, the front of my dress was ripped open and his mouth was on my skin.

"Oh," I moaned as his tongue trailed wet kisses to my nipples, teasing and driving me insane with desire.

"You're so beautiful," he whispered, cupping my breasts as his mouth moved upwards. When I realized where he stopped, I tensed up, wondering what would happen next.

Was he actually going to bite me? And worse, would I care?

His tongue stroked the skin near my collarbone and then moved up towards my ear, nibbling and licking. As I began to relax, his right hand released my breast and his fingers moved down my ribcage, across my bellybutton to my panties, stopping right at the edge of the cotton.

"Invite me in," he whispered against my neck.

"Yes…" I whispered, my legs trembling.

He ran one of his fingers over the top of the material and I gasped. "Say it…" he demanded.

"Come in, Ethan…"

Just as his fingers began to slide under the fabric, the door burst open and he shot up. His face was a mask of monstrous rage and my heart stopped as I saw his fangs for the first time. "What is the meaning of this?!" he growled.

Sheriff Caleb stood facing us while I pulled the blankets over my exposed body. His face was burning red, as were his homicidal eyes. "Why in the fuck did you bring her here?!"

Chapter Twenty-Four

They'd locked me in the bedroom but I could still hear their angry shouts from somewhere in the house. Caleb said he had to bring me back, but Ethan raged that I belonged with him. I wanted to go home desperately and prayed that Ethan would give in and release me.

There was a soft knock at the door and then it opened. An attractive red-haired girl entered the room, who I only assumed was Celeste, Caleb's daughter. This time she wasn't wearing glasses and her startling green eyes stared at me with interest.

"Here," she said, throwing me a pair of shorts and T-shirt. "I heard you needed this."

I stared at her, wondering if she was a vampire, too.

"Yes," she said with a sardonic grin. "I am whatever it is you think I am."

"What, you can read minds?" I asked.

She laughed. "No, I could tell what you were thinking by the expression on your face."

"What are they going to do with me?" I asked.

"If Ethan had his way, you'd never leave his side. Caleb doesn't really trust you, but he has the hots for your mom and isn't willing to hurt her."

I scowled. "How fucking sensitive of him."

She laughed. "So, what do *you* want to do?" she asked. "Do you care for Ethan?"

"I don't know," I said, pulling the T-shirt over my head, "he stares into my eyes and I want nothing more than to be with him. But that's not real, is it? Isn't that some kind of power he has to control people?"

She nodded. "True."

"But, even now…" I said. "He has this effect on me and he's not even in the room. I guess I really might feel something for him. It's all so confusing."

"It's only natural to feel lust towards him, if that's all it is. He's very sexy."

"That is no lie."

"Caleb said he caught you with some guy named Duncan," she said.

"Yeah," I answered. "I've kind of been seeing Duncan."

"Are you in love with this, Duncan?"

"I think I'm confused. I don't know. Maybe I'm a little in love with both of them."

She smiled. "Being in love with one of us is dangerous. If you decide to stay with Ethan, you can't live a normal life."

I swallowed. "So, are you vampires?"

She grimaced. "I never did like that word."

I swallowed. "So… do you suck people's blood?"

She stepped closer to me and touched my cheek as I held my breath. "We take nourishment wherever we can get it. Some are willing to give us our nourishment, some don't have much say in the matter."

I backed up. "So, you are willing to kill people if you have to?"

166

She smiled darkly. "Survival of the fittest."

"Is Caleb turning my mother into one of you?"

"I believe that he has chosen your mother to be his mate."

Oh, hell.

"Is Caleb your real father?" I asked, continuing with my questions. If she was willing to answer, I wasn't going to stop.

"Yes," she said. "My father became a… vampire first. He then turned me into one to save my life."

My eyebrows shot up. "What do you mean?"

"I had Typhoid."

"Wow, when was that?"

"Eighteen ninety-one," she said.

I stared at her in shock. "That would make you…"

"Much older than you," she answered.

Caleb stormed into the bedroom and waved at me. "Let's go. We have to get you out of here before your brother and Duncan show up. I guess they know about this place from Susan."

"Are you taking me home?" I asked, backing away from him.

His eyes narrowed. "You weren't hurt, and when I walked in on you and Ethan, you looked to be enjoying yourself. You aren't planning on pressing any charges against Ethan, are you?"

I looked past Caleb to where Ethan was standing with his arms crossed, looking furious. "No," I said.

"You aren't going to make any trouble for us, are you? Not that anyone would believe you anyway," said Caleb.

"If you leave my mother alone," I said. "I'll keep my mouth shut."

Caleb's face turned dark. "I can't do that."

"Yes you can! Do you think I want my mom turning into a vampire? I've seen her neck!" I yelled, surprising myself.

167

He sighed. "There are things you don't understand. Your mother… I have feelings for her and I'd do anything for her."

"So you'd turn her into one of you?"

He ran a hand through his hair. "How do I say this?" he stepped closer. "Your mother has cancer and I'm giving her a second chance."

I snorted. "You seriously expect me to believe that?"

"She has breast cancer," he said, his face grim. "Hell, she doesn't even know about it yet."

I felt sick to my stomach. "What, you can sense that?"

He nodded. "Yes and if she becomes one of us, she'll survive. If she doesn't, she may die."

"But you didn't even consider giving her a chance?"

"I was afraid she'd say no," he said. "You're right, though, I didn't give her a choice. She may hate me when she finds out, but at least she'll be alive."

"Do you consider yourself alive?"

Ethan stepped past Caleb and put his hands on my shoulders. "Do I look dead to you? What you felt earlier, was that really so bad?"

I stepped back. "Ethan, you're trying to control me again. I don't know how I feel about you because it isn't real. You use your powers to make me feel things that I'm not even sure about."

"I only did it the first night we met," he said. "And I'm…. sorry. But I haven't manipulated you at all since that night. Every feeling, every emotion you've had since then, has been real."

There was a sharp knock at the door and someone stepped into the room. "We have to do something, now!" hollered one of the guys I'd seen Ethan with in the diner the other night. "Someone's here. I think it's her damn brother."

"Fuck," groaned Caleb.

"Wait," said Celeste. "Let *me* take care of him."

168

"Don't you dare hurt my brother," I snapped.

She smiled. "Believe me, when I'm done with him, he'll be begging me to hurt him. But in a good way."

I wasn't sure what she meant, but Caleb nodded and said, "Celeste won't hurt him or she'll answer to me."

She gave him a pouty face as she stepped out of the room.

Caleb nodded towards the door. "You're free to leave," he said to me.

I looked at Ethan, who was obviously upset. "I…"

"I told you before that you were free to go," he said. "I'd never do anything to hurt you."

I'm sure he still thought I was Miranda and wanted me to become a vampire like he was. But the very idea of doing that was frightening beyond belief. I still wasn't exactly sure how I felt about him, but I knew without a doubt that I didn't belong to that world.

I looked down and stepped past him to the door.

"Nikki."

I turned to him. "What, Ethan?"

"You haven't seen the last of me."

I wish I could have pretended that those words didn't affect me, but they did. He must have noticed my reaction, because he licked his lips and gave me a slow sexy smile.

"Goodbye, Ethan," I said, walking away.

Chapter Twenty-Five

They lived in a large old colonial that was very well furnished. I'm not sure why I was so surprised; if they were vampires and could live for centuries, they had time to save for such luxuries.

"Nikki!" hollered my brother from the front door. "Are you okay?"

I was walking down a long spiral staircase that faced the front door where Nathan and Duncan stood. They were being held back by two other guys from the diner, who I assumed were also vampires. Celeste was also with them.

"I'm fine," I said.

Duncan looked pissed and was glaring at the vampires. "Get out of our way so we can make sure she's not hurt!"

"Now, now," said Celeste. "She's doing fine. She came here on her own free will, and isn't hurt in the least."

"Who are you?" asked Duncan.

She smiled. "I'm a friend of Nikki's and Anne's. I'm Caleb's daughter, Celeste."

"She's fine," confirmed Caleb, trying to ease the tension in the room. "And she's not pressing charges because she came on her own free will."

I walked to the front door and Duncan put his arms around me. "Are you okay?" he asked, searching my face.

"Yeah, I'm fine."

Duncan frowned and looked at Caleb. "I should press charges against that asshole, Ethan, wherever he is."

"I'm right here," said Ethan, coming down from the top of the stairs.

"Okay, do you want to press charges?" asked Caleb.

Duncan glared at Ethan, who was smiling malevolently. "I just want him to leave Nikki alone," he said.

"Nikki and I are friends," replied Ethan, his eyes undressing me again. Even now I wanted to be underneath him, his mouth and hands everywhere. Especially when he looked at me that way – like I was his possession and he knew it.

"Right," snapped Duncan.

"I remember you now," said Celeste to Nathan. "You're the cute guy from the grocery store the other night."

Nathan's eyes appeared to dilate as he stared at the beautiful vampire. A lopsided grin spread across his face. "I was wondering what happened to you. It's nice to see you again."

"And it's *very* nice to see you," she replied, twirling a red curl around her finger.

Duncan frowned. "Nathan, she's with them. Don't fall for this shit."

Nathan ignored him, staring at her as if she was a buffet of food and he was dying of starvation. "So, Celeste, what are you doing with these jackasses?"

"I rode over here with my dad," she answered. "I'm friends with Ethan and wanted to find out what was happening." She looked at Duncan and smiled. "You must be Duncan?"

Duncan sighed. "Yeah."

"I've heard all about you," she said, putting her hands on her hips. "Nikki's quite fond of you."

He looked at me and I smiled.

Celeste yawned. "Guys, I'm getting *really* tired and I think everyone should go home now, it's very late. Isn't that right, Duncan?"

Duncan's eyes dilated as their eyes met. "Yes, it's getting late. We should all go home."

"Good thinking," she said with an amused expression. She turned to Caleb who looked satisfied at the change of events. "Daddy, I'm starving. Can we stop somewhere for a late snack on the way home?"

From the look in her eyes, I knew her snack wasn't the type I'd enjoy. I quickly grabbed Duncan's and Nathan's hands. "We have to leave. *Now.*"

"Goodbye, Nikki," called Ethan. "I'm sure I'll be seeing you very soon."

Duncan somehow snapped out of his trance. He stared at Ethan with hate. "Stay the fuck away from her!"

"Only if she wants me to," he replied, his eyes still focused on me.

That had nothing to do with what I wanted from him. In fact, I knew that if we didn't get out of the house soon, I'd never be able to leave. "Let's go," I said, pulling them through the door.

When we got into Nathan's Mustang, his mind seemed to clear from whatever spell Celeste had put him under. "What in the hell just happened?"

"I don't know," said Duncan, who was sitting in the backseat, tapping his fingers nervously on the door. "What I do know is that I should have had Ethan arrested for trying to kill me earlier."

"Are you sure you're okay, Nikki?" asked my brother. "You weren't bitten or anything, were you?"

I shook my head.

172

"So, is Ethan a vampire or what?" asked Duncan. "He certainly has some kind of super strength. He almost killed me on the beach. Then he took off with my girl. I feel like such a lame excuse for a boyfriend. "

I turned around to look at him. "There's no way you could have done anything more. And look, I'm here, now, and I'm totally fine."

He sighed. "It's my fault, you know. You warned me about walking on the beach. I'm just glad you're okay. I was so worried that he might have killed you or something."

"No, he wouldn't kill me."

"How can you be so sure? You can't trust that maniac. Look what happened to Abigail."

"We don't know if he did that," I said, not wanting to believe it. I couldn't imagine Ethan as a murderer. Not when he made me feel so safe and alive.

"Did you actually ask him?" asked Nathan.

"Um, no. Are you kidding?"

He frowned. "What about those other girls. Did you ask him about those?"

"No."

The truth was, I was terrified of his answer.

"So, what were you doing all this time?" asked Duncan.

I lied. "Just talked about other things." I certainly couldn't tell him the truth. It did neither of us any good, and until I figured out what had actually happened and whether or not I'd had any control, I'd keep it to myself. Besides, hurting Duncan was the last thing I wanted to do. "To tell you the truth, I talked to Celeste more than anyone."

"She is so freaken hot," said Nathan, grinning. "I'm going to have to get her number from Caleb."

"No, Nathan. Just stay away from her," I said.

"Why?" asked Nathan. "Because you don't like Caleb?"

I sighed. "No, because she's a *vampire*. So is he, by the way."

Nathan slammed on the brakes. "What?"

Before I could continue, something landed on the top of Nathan's car with a loud thud.

"Shit!" hollered Duncan as Ethan jumped to the ground. "He's come back for Nikki."

The doors were locked but it didn't stop him. He ripped mine open and tossed it into the ditch.

"Shit, no... he didn't just do that to my Mustang!" hollered Nathan, getting out of the car.

"Hi," smiled Ethan, as he bent down on one knee. He held out his hand to me. "I just couldn't stay away. Do you have a few minutes to talk in private?"

"No," I said, backing away. "I can't go anywhere with you."

He actually looked hurt. He stood up. "Why?"

"Leave her alone, you bastard!" snarled Duncan, getting out of the car. He walked around and stood next to Nathan, his fists clenched, ready to fight.

"I think we can take him together, bro," said Nathan, taking a step towards Ethan.

Ethan smiled with a hint of fang. "I won't hurt you because Nikki wants it that way. But if either of you touch me, your future holds no promises."

"Okay, fine, what do you want with me?" I asked, getting out of the car. I didn't want anyone hurt but from the look on everyone's faces, something was about to go down. Unfortunately, there was no doubt in my mind that it would be Duncan and Nathan.

Ethan sighed and ran a hand through his black hair, which was still messy from rolling around in bed with me. "I'm leaving. Caleb has banished me and I'm going to New York."

174

"Good," replied Duncan. "Then you'd better move quickly, daylight's coming."

He smiled coldly. "Daylight doesn't affect me. It's just a little… uncomfortable."

"My sister isn't going anywhere with you," said Nathan. "And guess what? You're going to pay for my door before you leave."

Ethan took out his wallet and threw several hundred dollar bills at his feet. "There you go, *bro*. Get it fixed."

"Asshole," mumbled Nathan, picking up the bills.

Ethan turned back to me. "Can we just have a little time alone, Nikki? There are some things I need to tell you."

Duncan moved in front of me. "You stay the fuck away from her."

"This doesn't concern you," replied Ethan, glaring at Duncan. "Move aside."

"You're going to have to make me," he growled.

I groaned and stepped around him. "Fine, I'll talk to you, Ethan." If he actually was leaving, I wanted to find out what he had to say.

"Bullshit," said Nathan. "No way is that going to happen."

I turned to my brother and grabbed his arm, pulling him away. "Nathan," I whispered. "Just, let me talk to him. He hasn't hurt me. Not ever. Give us a few minutes alone, within eyesight of you two. Maybe he'll give us information on those murders. I seriously don't think he did it but maybe he knows who did."

"No! He might sweep you away like he did last time," said Nathan. "Besides, what do you have to say to this… monster?"

I stared into his eyes. "Nathan, nothing is going to happen, okay? Just, trust me. We won't go far, and if I need your help, I'll call you guys. Please?"

"What's going on?" asked Duncan, moving closer to us.

175

He rubbed his forehead. "She really wants to talk to Ethan."

Duncan's eyes widened in alarm. "Why?"

"To see if he knows anything about those murders. Trust me, he won't hurt me."

"It's him I don't trust," grunted Duncan.

"I could have taken her already," volunteered Ethan loudly. Obviously, his ears were picking up on our conversation. "But I haven't and won't, if that's her decision."

"What about the mind control thing? He might talk you into it," said Nathan.

I turned towards Ethan. "You *won't* use that. Right, Ethan?" I asked, raising my voice, although I didn't know what the point was.

"Of course not."

"I still don't like it," said Duncan, advancing towards Ethan. "She's my girl, asshole. Why can't you leave her alone?"

Ethan ignored him. He held his hand out to me as I chased after Duncan, to stop him. "Nikki? Can we just have a few moments alone? Seriously, I don't have much time."

"Yes," I replied, ignoring his hand. I knew my brother and Duncan were still angry, but I wanted to hear what Ethan had to say.

"Don't worry, I'll take good care of her," said Ethan right before he grabbed my hand and flew away.

Chapter Twenty-Six

"Ethan!" I shouted as soon as we landed. I stepped away and pointed at him angrily. "What the hell? You weren't supposed to actually fly off with me like that!"

"I wanted to be alone with you. It might be our last time," he pouted.

I sighed. "That wasn't supposed to be part of the deal."

"Sorry."

"So, what is this about?"

He smiled. "I wanted you to come with me. To New York."

My eyes widened. "I'm still in school and you're a... vampire. I can't just go away with you."

He got down on his knees and stared up at me. "Would it help if I confessed my undead love for you?"

This time I laughed out loud. "You're crazy."

He stood up and pulled me back into his arms. "Hey, the only thing I'm crazy about, is you."

"I'm not so sure about that. I mean, you keep calling me Miranda. I'm not this person and I'll never be her."

He tipped my chin up and stared into my eyes. "I know that. Look, Nikki, I'm drawn to you, and as far as I'm concerned, nothing else matters."

"Drawn to me?"

"Yes. There's this magnetic pull between us, can't you feel it? It's like, we were meant to be together."

"I don't know about a magnetic pull... I mean, I like you. I like you, a lot. But..."

"But what? Just throw caution to the wind. I'll take care of you, Nikki. I swear I'll keep you safe."

"I just can't do what you're asking. My mother needs me so much right now, and I can't leave my brother. You have to understand that? You and I... we don't even really know each other."

"I won't force you to come with me, but I want you to understand that I can't come back to this place."

I stared at his face, which was so incredibly handsome. I knew I'd miss him. Whether it was real or not, I felt something for Ethan and wished things were different.

He bent forward and pressed his lips to mine.

"Your skin, it's so cool," I whispered, touching his cheek.

"I haven't had time to... feed. I had other things on my mind."

I touched his forehead. "When your skin is cooler, does it mean you're weaker?"

"Yes, In fact, I'll lose most of my strength if I don't eat soon. That's another reason I wanted to move quickly."

"So, what exactly do you need to... survive?"

He smiled bitterly. "Do you really want to know?"

"Not really, but I need to know one thing; do you kill innocent people?"

He shook his head vehemently. "No. I feed off of willing victims. I only take what I need and they live to see another day. Swear to God."

178

I stared at him. I wasn't sure where he found 'willing victims' and wasn't about to ask.

I sighed. "Where are you going to find a willing victim now?"

"I don't know yet," he smiled grimly. "I guess I hadn't thought about that when I was chasing after you. I just really wanted to see you before I left."

"How about me?"

His eyes widened. "You?"

I pulled my hair away from my neck. "Yes, use my blood. Do it before I change my mind, though."

He stared at my neck and licked his lips. "I... there is some danger involved. If anything happened to you, I'd never forgive myself."

"Then you'd better do it quickly, before I chicken out. I hate needles enough as it is."

He lips curled up. "It's not quite the same thing."

I swallowed. "Okay, does it hurt?"

He caressed my neck with his fingertip and I shivered. "I can make it enjoyable for you," he whispered, huskily.

I looked up into his blue eyes and the naked desire reflected there made me breathless. "Okay," I whispered. "Just do it, quickly."

"You sure?"

"Yes. Take my blood."

His eyes dilated. With a low growl in the back of his throat, his lips crushed mine and his tongue made its way into my mouth, stroking and demanding a response.

And respond I did.

I slid my hands around his neck, drawing him closer and I could feel his arousal pressing against me. I shivered in delight as a desire to wrap my legs around his waist and hold on forever washed over me.

Instead, he let me go.

"Are you sure about this?" he asked. He was breathing so heavily, it reminded me of a lion panting for water.

I touched his lip with the pad of my thumb. It was so sensual and yet, something lurked behind it that both frightened and excited me. "Yes, just do it already."

Ethan stared into my eyes and a burning desire to do whatever he wanted, slammed through every nerve in my body. This time I grabbed the back of his head and pulled him down to meet my lips, feeling like I just couldn't get enough of his mouth.

He groaned against my lips and cupped my rear, rubbing his hips against mine, causing a warm ache between my legs. Just when I didn't think I could take it anymore, he raised his head.

"Please," I begged, not even sure of what I was asking for anymore.

He moved his mouth to my neck and paused. I could feel the coolness of his breath against my skin; I could also feel him trembling. "I love you," he whispered and then, his teeth broke through.

I shuddered in ecstasy as my blood flowed into him with a rush of pleasure so great, that I could have died and it wouldn't have mattered. "Ethan," I breathed, clutching him tighter so that I wouldn't fall.

A gunshot echoed through the night and suddenly he was backing away from me, a look of horror and pain etched on his face. Before I could ask him what had happened, he was gone.

"Did you get him?!" shouted my mother's voice in the darkness.

"Yeah," said Caleb. "He's bleeding. He won't get far."

My mother was crying hysterically as she rushed towards me. "Nikki! Oh, my God, you're bleeding everywhere. We have to get her to the hospital!" she screamed at Caleb.

Caleb nodded. "I've already called an ambulance."

"Mom," I whispered, staring at her in confusion. How did she get there? Where was Ethan?

"Are you okay?" she asked.

"Yeah... I'm... fine."

She shook her head and sobbed harder. "No, you're not! You're bleeding and you're so pale. Dear Lord, what was that monster doing to my little girl?!"

I couldn't answer her, because at that moment, I lost consciousness.

***

End of Book One
Book Two (Shiver) Now Available!

Kristen Middleton

SHIVER

Night Roamers: Book Two

Other stories by Kristen Middleton

Paranormal Young Adult
Zombie Games Origins (Free)
Zombie Games Running Wild
Zombie Games Dead Endz
Zombie Games Road Kill

Enchanted Secrets
Blur
Shiver
Vengeance

By K.L. Middleton (Contemporary Romance)
Tangled Beauty
Tangled Mess
Sharp Edges

www.kristenmiddleton.com

Made in the USA
Lexington, KY
28 February 2015